I0570974

Wide, Wild, Everywhere

Also by Alexandria Nolan

PARADISE OF EXILES

SHEARS OF FATE

Wide, Wild, Everywhere

Alexandria Nolan

Copyright © 2014 Alexandria Nolan

All rights reserved.

ISBN: 0615924751
ISBN-13:978-0615924755

DEDICATION

To all those who wander, who people watch, who imagine the lives of their fellow travelers. For those who wonder what life would be like if you lived in whatever city you visited.

For those of us whose minds run wild thinking how much different our lives would be if we could just live in a new place... and the realization that it would be mostly the same.

For the common thread amongst us all that we *would rather be anywhere than right where we are*. And for the opportunity to vacate your own existence for a short while and pretend to be someone, somewhere else in the world.

The question, O me! so sad, recurring—What good
  amid these, O me, O life?

Answer.

That you are here—that life exists and identity,
That the powerful play goes on,
and you may contribute a verse.

From"*O Me! O Life*" *Leaves of Grass*, Walt Whitman

CONTENTS

ACKNOWLEDGMENTS

A big thank you to all of the lovely (and not so lovely) people that we've had the pleasure of meeting on our travels. To wander and encounter people living in a totally different place, with completely varied experiences from our own, and STILL realize that we are basically all the same; this is a beautiful, wonderful, heartbreaking revelation. It is a realization that connects us all irrevocably... Aad sometimes tears us apart. This book is the product of many years of people watching and imagining what their lives might hold, attempting to capture the secrets of each of their hearts–the struggles that are individual, but also universal.

With appreciation and gratitude for your kindness and continued friendship. Especially Maria, Amber & Joshua.

Thank you to my parents, for encouragement, marketing strategy and letting me know when something 'just wasn't working'.

And of course, for TJN. The best and only person I can imagine exploring with.

"Some tourists think Amsterdam is a city of sin, but in truth it is a city of freedom. And in freedom, most people find sin." — John Green, *The Fault in Our Stars*

1 : AMSTERDAM

It wasn't that Peter didn't like Tyler. It wasn't that. It was just that Tyler was often obnoxious, embarrassing and loud. He was the only other guy that he could find to go on this trip though. The only guy with the means and the time off. Besides, he wasn't *all* bad. His blunt honesty could be refreshing, and he had never been unkind to Peter.

It was difficult though, to be on this trip, without Allison. They'd planned it last year and booked it all together. Peter remembered her face, lit up like a birthday party, as they received the confirmation e-mail. But then she'd met Simon and left him, and not even a trip to

"The Venice of the North" could make her stay. Poor Tyler had that against him from the start. Well, the man could hardly help not being Allison.

Peter had decided to make the best of an awkward situation. If only Tyler could be less...conspicuous. He was always talking to everyone, over-sharing, giving out details that Peter didn't want strangers to know. Details, that in the wrong ears could be dangerous for people to know about them.

Peter had known Tyler for years. They had met in college and had gone to the same parties, had the same friends, but had never been all that close themselves. Peter was a private person, never needing to ruffle feathers or challenge others. If he differed in opinion from someone, he felt no need to defend it or debate it. He was comfortable with himself. Comfortable in his own opinions. Some might say cold, or calculatin, that was definitely what Allison had said. "Cut off from the world", "Indifferent to others", these had been the stabbing arrows in her arsenal. Tyler, was much different. He wore his heart on his sleeve, and always felt the need to explain all of his thoughts. He was always questioning, talking and declaring. It was exhausting.

But, after Allison left, he still had this trip. It was paid for, besides the plane ticket that couldn't be switched. He was bent on going, but when he called around, he realized that somehow in the last five years of his Allison odyssey, all of his friends had gotten married, had children, and were living comfortably in the suburbs. How had he missed that step? He realized that not only was he behind, he wasn't even on the same staircase.

But then his old roommate, Heath, had suggested Tyler. According to Heath, Ty was always traveling and hadn't a family of his own yet either. So, even though they had always been merely, "friend of a friend", when Peter called, Tyler agreed immediately. He'd never been to Amsterdam before.

So here they were. Touring the Heineken factory, peering into canals, looking into the museums in Museumplein, and hitting the bars in Leidseplein. For the most part, Tyler had turned out to be an eager and friendly travel companion, albeit a somewhat disagreeable one.

For now though, Peter was focused on savoring the moments and exploring the city. It seemed so alive and he felt that he immediately fit there. Peter traveled often, but there was always that strange, nagging foreign feeling. As if one did not quite belong. It was always apparent on his trips, no matter how much he would seek to immerse himself into another culture, he somehow stuck out, or felt he did. But not here. Here, he could imagine himself riding his bike to work, never tiring of these stately and friendly canal houses.

It was one of the few things they agreed on. Tyler couldn't seem to get enough of Amsterdam either. Using the broken Dutch he'd picked up from bothering their servers in restaurants or shop employees, he'd converse with anyone that gave him a second glance. But he went too far. When he came out with that stupid skull cap, with "AMSTERDAM" emblazoned in annoying knitted letters, Peter had enough. But, getting angry wasn't his style. Not out loud anyway. He simply grit his teeth and continued walking down the streets, staring at everything except Tyler and his stupid hat. Every few minutes, he would glance back up at Tyler, and he had the same idiotic smile on his face. Like a child. It was no surprise to Peter that his companion was still single. What woman in their right mind would marry him?

That night, they left their hotel, near the Pijp. It had been a great choice-Allison's choice in fact. It was a bustling area mostly filled with young people, many of them university students. The area had street fairs and local food, such as the raw herring the city was known for. Tyler had chatted up the waitress at the restaurant they'd had breakfast at this morning, and she had told them that two great shows were playing at both the Melkweg and Paradiso clubs in the Leidseplein. Peter realized that Tyler's incessant conversation did yield some great tourist information, but he wasn't to admit that to Tyler.

That night, swaying in the darkness of the club, he found himself caught up in the moment. The music pounded into Peter's body. He forgot to be reserved. He was dancing, and buying drinks and talking to all of the girls. He didn't even know if they were pretty, and he didn't care. He was high-fiving Tyler and found himself singing along with the rest of the Dutch when the band decided to play an old Andre Hazes song. The club erupted with the voices of all within, and although neither of the Americans knew the words, they were crying and yelling out some kind of lyrics. Lights, music, the sweat on his body from dancing, dancing, dancing. Peter was in love with life, and with Tyler and Amsterdam. He was kissing someone. He loved her! Now she was gone, and he was kissing someone else. Now he was feeling sick, and the lights were dimming. Everything was fuzzy, then dim, then all was darkness.

Peter awoke the next morning in his own bed, back in their hotel room. He was wearing a pair of basketball shorts and the same t-shirt he had worn to the bar. The room was spinning, and his stomach felt as if a gnawing hole was inside of it. How did he get here? Where was Tyler? Tyler's bed was made, and there was no sign of him. Peter didn't take much time to think about it, as he shifted to his side, closed his eyes firmly, and sank back into the dizzying darkness of his own tortured body.

He awoke again, hours later. He didn't know how he knew that hours had gone by, but he could feel it. Slowly, he sat up in bed and allowed the angles of his room to sharpen into focus. He found a ligonberry muffin, a banana and a large cup of water next to his bed. He picked them each up in turn, inspecting them, smelling them, not able to immediately determine if they were real. Would Tyler have done this for him? Peter flushed with shame. This man he had held in contempt, whom he had judged and sneered at. Whom he had merely thought of as a person to split the cost of the trip- this man had cared for him and kept him safe in a foreign place. The shame surged within him again. Like a hot knife, searing through his conscience. The shame of drinking too much, of losing control, of having to rely on someone else, of worrying about how badly he had acted. Perhaps Allison had been right. Peter was cold. He was shut off. Reaching up to run his fingers through his thick, black hair, he stretched and got up. He grabbed the muffin, and as he swallowed he felt the void in his stomach filling, healing.

With his other hand he was gulping down the water, it went down awkwardly, like a drowning man whose mouth is filling with water although it chokes him to drink it. He looked into the mirror in the bathroom. What was this face? Who was this man? He looked deeply into his dark, almost black eyes and his dark olive skin, that now seemed slightly yellow from the alcohol, and the dark circles under his eyes were so deep they almost frightened him. Peter prided himself on his coloring, and it had all but been destroyed in his attempts to forget himself the night before.

He had spent so much time distancing himself from other people, and then last night. Last night, he had felt happy. He had felt alive and in the moment. It wasn't just the alcohol, it was the abandon. It was, unbelievably, Tyler. Tyler who had no judgements for him, who was always curious and friendly and embarrassingly kind to everyone.

The door to their hotel room opened, and in walked Tyler. He smiled at Peter and said he had just been out buying souvenirs for his mother and his kid sister, Josie. He asked Peter how he was feeling, and waved off any thanks of helping him into bed, or bringing him food and water. His reply had been, "Oh, you would have done the same for me, I expect". Which had made Peter wonder, would he? He was ashamed to admit to himself that he probably would not. They discussed dinner, and Peter said he would be down in the lobby in an hour or so, after showering and making himself presentable. Then Tyler left, to drink some fresh mint tea, and read over and reply to some e-mails his company had sent him.

An hour or so later, Peter stepped off the elevator, and caught Tyler's smiling face across the room. For a moment, the sight of his perpetual grin was irritating, but, catching his thoughts, he silently cursed himself for his ugly judgement. They walked easily together, down the street and caught a tram to the restaurant they had decided on. They both seemed lost in their own thoughts, and rode along, unspeaking but pleasantly, until their stop. It was an organic, healthy foods restaurant that specialized in soup, salads and raw juices. Peter knew that Tyler suggested it because Peter had been poorly all day, and was grateful for his thoughtfulness. The same feelings of shame coursed through him, at the thought of how arrogant and hurtful he had been towards this extraordinarily kind person.

And then they talked. Really talked. They discussed their college days, and laughed over the memories of the night before. They threw out suggestions for their last few days in the city. Tyler flirted with the woman behind the counter mercilessly until she was giggling and wagging a finger at him, but also looking back with a smile when he wasn't looking. Peter took a good look at Tyler, as if seeing him for the first time. He was taller, at least 6'4", which made him fit right in with all of the giants here in the Netherlands. He gave one the impression of lankiness and recklessness. His blonde hair was clean and well cut, but fell carelessly in place. His eyes were piercing blue and his cheeks were rosy with warmth and kindness. He was like a tall, gangling, cherub. That same face that had made Peter's skin crawl, now looked different. It seemed genuine, and loving.

Peter then made an offhand comment about how strange he had found it to discover their whole graduating class was married and had children. He was smiling at Tyler, he thought communicating goodwill and camaraderie, but for a moment he could have sworn that Tyler's face fell into gloom. Just as soon as the wave of emotion had settled, however, it was gone. Tyler replied, "Well, we should move here then. Nobody here would even think of being married at our age".

"How do you mean?"

"Well, here, they believe that Americans are always rushing too much. That we are makers of our own unhappiness. That we do everything too fast. I can't help but agree. Our decisions are always made in such haste, and then we rush on to the next unhappiness."

Peter was stunned. This sudden outburst of thought had to have the most depth of any conversation they'd ever had. Peter found himself explaining about Allison, and how she'd left him for someone that she'd just met. He poured his soul out to Tyler over pumpkin soup and beet salad. Tyler's comment had stirred something inside of him. It wasn't Allison's hasty decision that had got him thinking, it was his slow, callous decision to exclude people from his feelings. He had so easily decided on his own unhappiness, and he wasn't sure where it started. In college?

Suddenly, Peter realized that he didn't remember ever seeing Tyler after their junior year. They had both been in the business program, albeit different specialties, but he still should have ran into him. Had he been that focused on Allison and on finishing his degree that he didn't remember?

But when Peter inquired where he had been hiding their senior year, the same pained look cast a shadow over Tyler's face. This time it remained. His hand came up to cover his mouth and his eyes closed, his whole head facing down towards his half-eaten bowl of greens. Finally, he looked up and looked right into Peter's eyes. In the most serious voice Peter could have imagined him taking on, he calmly asked, "Why exactly did you ask me to come on this trip? And what all did they tell you about what happened?"

Peter was aghast. He wasn't sure how to respond. Tyler's face shifted. No longer was he the sweet, fun-loving, bumbling ox of a man that he had been for the duration of their trip, instead he was faced with someone he recognized. Peter looked into Tyler's eyes, and for a moment saw himself. The coldness, the distrust of friendliness, the gnawing sadness. Things he had felt in himself, but had never admitted were truly there—even as they consumed him. Peter's eyes, went wide, and when he opened his mouth to explain, he stammered. He finally got out that he asked him to come because no one else could, and that he had no idea what he was talking about–he had heard nothing.

Either the words, his expression or a combination of both seemed to satisfy Tyler. He turned and looked out the front windows of the restaurant into the street. Peter's eyes followed his, and they both sat silently for a moment, watching a woman walk by with a stroller, a little girl skipping along beside. The woman must have known the owner of the restaurant they were in, because she looked right into the windows, and waved at the proprietor who was standing some steps behind their table. Then, taking hold of the little girl's hand again, they proceeded briskly down the sidewalk. Tyler's eyes came back to meet Peter's. He spoke.

"Listen Pete, I know we didn't know each other that well in college, but I liked you. I heard you were smart, and funny and a good guy to play a gag on someone with. But, I think we both know we weren't close. Is it safe to say you didn't know my personality in college, and that you were surprised when we met up to leave for this trip?"

Tyler waited a moment for Peter to nod his head in agreement, and then taking another swig of the bright green juice in front of him, continued on.

"I was a lot different back then. I was a little how you describe yourself now. I was shut off. I was worried about my family and my grades and my friends. I had a girlfriend back home, Miranda. She was two years younger than me in school, and she was the sweetest thing you've ever met. I swear to God. She thought I was the most spectacular guy in the world, and when someone thinks you're that special, it's hard not to see yourself that way, too. But I was in college. I liked to drink. I wanted to party and be wild and I liked to hurt people. I cheated on her all the time...I slept with a different girl as often as I could. I even slept with a couple of girls in your ex-girlfriend Allison's sorority. I know that because I saw you sneaking out of that sorority house a time or two, same as me. I was young and selfish, ya know? Well, Miranda was sweet as pie, but she wasn't stupid. She found out. She came up to my apartment while I was in class to surprise me, and found whatever proof she needed. Instead of admitting it, or apologizing though, I...I treated her like she was nothing. I cut her off stone cold. I told her she 'didn't understand college', that she 'didn't understand me'. "

Tyler stopped for a moment. Peter was bewildered. Where was this story going? Why was he telling him all of this? Tyler took a deep breath that almost sounded like a sob, and continued,
"She'd had a miscarriage. I hadn't seen her since Christmas break, and she had come to visit me and tell me. She hadn't even known she was pregnant until she lost the baby. But, she didn't get the chance to tell me. I had shut myself right off from her. I had completely cut her off. She went home and killed herself, Pete. I killed her. I killed this beautiful, sweet, trusting, girl with my

thoughtlessness and dishonesty. I killed her with my deceit and selfishness. And now, I carry her with me everywhere. She's with me all the time. Pulling on my sleeve, prompting me to be kind. Reminding me to listen to people, to make them smile, to be open and honest. I see her easy smile on every girl's face. I see her trust. I didn't want her around, and now I look for her everywhere."

He sat back from the table as if it had been an enormous effort to tell Peter all of this. He explained further that he had taken a year off of school, and then came back and finished up after the rest of us had graduated. Peter couldn't believe that this big, goofy, smiling man across from him was carrying around the weight of that sadness. And that instead of giving into that darkness, he forced himself to bring kindness and light to everyone he talked to. Everyone. Whether or not they held him in contempt, or judged him or behaved as if he was a half-wit, he had learned the price of ugliness and thoughtlessness .

Peter saw him with new eyes. This bumbling idiot that he had held in such disdain seemed so much more complex, there were so many more curves and angles to his personality. There was so much more to people than what appeared. Everyone was plunged into the depths of their own secret sorrows, their own prejudices, we were all drowning in a sea of our own bad decisions or regrets. How easy it was to cut yourself off from others. From rejection. How much easier to judge those around you than to try and love them. Isn't that exactly what Peter had done?

The owner came to their table then and asked about the food, the serious look fell from Tyler's face and a smile appeared, easy and genuine. Kindness beamed from both of them, as if it was a germ that Tyler was spreading. Tyler murmured a few Dutch words he'd picked up, and obviously strung them together incorrectly, but it made the owner laugh and put a hand on Tyler's shoulder. Peter smiled at both of them, feeling the possibilities that genuine joy brings. Feeling again, the abandon of the night before, the peace with all beings everywhere that only comes from kindness.

"But Paris was a very old city and we were young and nothing was simple there, not even poverty, nor sudden money, nor the moonlight, nor right and wrong nor the breathing of someone who lay beside you in the moonlight."—Ernest Hemingway, A Moveable Feast

2 : PARIS

Maggie gazed out the window of her hotel. Yes, her life was truly charmed. The fresh, bright, spring sunshine of Paris flooded her opulent room, and she fairly pinched herself that it was all real. From the window, which she had propped open, she could see the Eiffel Tower. That great, powerful symbol of all things romantic, posh and quintessentially Parisian. She giggled to herself, and dipped her hand into the soft green box and came out clutching two pale green pistachio macarons. They were Gerard's choice, and although they weren't her particular favorite, the flavor reminded her of him.

Where was he? She hadn't heard him get up out of bed this morning. He must have gone out to fetch them breakfasts or to pick her up some little thing that caught his eye that he knew she'd like. He was clever at that. He always knew what she wanted, even before she did. She smiled to herself, realizing that her style was probably easy to identify–she liked things shiny and expensive. He had left her the most darling little note. It read, "Do not be angry, mon cher. I have gone. Will you miss me? xx Gerard"

What a little devil he was! Her mind easily drifted back to the day they had met. She had come to Europe on holiday with her sorority sisters, they were making the European tour during the summer after graduating from college. Their last free summer before they would be forced to settle down and become perfectly boring adults, a role that Maggie was blissfully happy to put on hold. She was the family favorite, and she could really do no wrong. Her parents were completely proud of her brother Simon, but as fond as he was of her, he had been a terrible bore about her "being less selfish". He had admonished her right before she left about "being more appreciative for all that Mother and Father had given her". Well, that was very well for him, he seemed to like hard work, but no, the universe held something different for Maggie. She could feel it. Nowhere had she felt it more than on the bridge in Prague where she met Gerard.

Her friends had begun to get on her nerves.

None of them had hardly any money, not compared to Maggie anyway. She didn't understand why they would beg her to stay in hostels. Was it her fault that their pathetic parents didn't have the cash to help them see Europe "the right way?" She couldn't begin to understand their reluctance to spend their money on lavish nights out, or fancy new clothes. The way they were set on traveling seemed squalid to her. Dreadful. But when she and Gerard made eye contact on that windy day in the Czech Republic, she knew she'd found a kindred spirit.

He'd walked right up to her, brazenly. From the moment their eyes had met, he didn't break contact. He approached her, and in his marvelous French had begun speaking rapidly. She had giggled, and it must have been an American laugh, because he instantly switched to a delightful, lilting, heavily-accented English. Her friends had found him attractive, it was impossible to find him anything else. But they were also wary. Why was he so forward? Maggie was glad they had been shocked when she reciprocated his intensity. She had been more than happy to prove to Gerard that she was a cut above her silly friends. It hadn't taken long after that. She had left the unsuitable 3 star hotel in Prague that she had compromised on, and soon they were staying at only the best. Gerard had shared her belief in "doing things the right way", which of course had translated into sparing no expense. What was wrong with that? After all, she deserved it.

From Prague they had gone on through Vienna, then Berlin, and now Paris. She was so happy they were finally here. She dipped her hand back into the pale green box next to her, her eyes never leaving the sturdy form of the tower. Her hand emerged clutching a white macaron. She couldn't recall if it was coconut or vanilla flavored, and honestly didn't mind which it was. Wasn't life a beautiful dream?

She had been looking forward to Paris for many reasons. It wasn't just that the city of love was the perfect place for her and her beloved Gerard. That of course, went without saying. But it was also the location of Gerard's bank. Poor Gerard. He'd had such trouble throughout their time on the continent accessing his money. It was the only time she'd seen him upset. He would try to access his funds, have an issue, angrily call his bank and then reappear upset and tense. She would calm him down and console him. She would cover his face with soft kisses until he smiled again. Ahh, she loved the drama of it. It was almost like a movie, they would have a scene and then they'd embrace and declare their feelings, and hold on to each other tighter. He had plenty of money. It was obvious by his clothes, his watches, his mode of traveling. It was apparent in his tastes and attitude. She wasn't worried about it. Now that they were in Paris, he would be repaying her for all of the trinkets and gifts he had picked out for her on the tour. Even though it was her card, and her money that had actually paid for them, it was only temporary. He would be reimbursing her. He'd said she needed those things. That a princess like her should have all of the baubles and diamonds they could find. He'd been so upset when his bank had declined the purchase. No, he was right, she did deserve it. And now that he finally had access to his money, all of the gifts he had bought with her money would be repaid. Gosh, but he was wonderful. And handsome. And generous.

He was always so cool. So careless. His clothes hung off of his lean, muscular frame as if they had been designed for him alone, (and perhaps they were!) His dark hair was worn shaggy and it smelled like lavender. His facial hair was scruffy, yet well groomed. As if he had planned for it to look that way. Yes, indeed, he was handsome. Effortless. His eyes lit up into an easy smile. A European smile. Not the wide cheesy grins of American boys. No, this was the easy, seductive, sultry lift of the corners of the mouth that only someone who is acutely aware of his own powers of seduction is able to manage. A man's smile. Ahh, she could picture it perfectly. She could see that same smile as he had undressed her every night for their lovemaking.

And she? She had always considered herself brash and bold, but with him she felt like a ingenue. She felt like a perfect porcelain doll in his hands. She'd always been short, and petite with dark curls and a creamy complexion. In college she'd gone as "Sexy Snow White" every year for Halloween, but now she truly felt like she had been a sleeping maid in the forest, awakened now by the attentions of this amazing man. Yes, sleeping. Dozing from the tedium of a mediocre life with subpar expectations. It turned her stomach to think of all of sorority sisters she'd come on this trip with. They were all excited about their careers, and talked incessantly about their boring boyfriends, pathetic families and "making a difference in the world". Ugh. She felt nauseated.

Now she'd never need to be ordinary. They would all be (even more) jealous of her. They would all lament that their lives didn't hold more for them. She'd show her stupid brother Simon with his dreary job. She'd flaunt her happiness in front of her overworked parents. She couldn't wait for everyone's reaction when she, Margaret Ashley O'Shea, brought the world to its knees.

She smirked inwardly, she so loved to indulge these wicked plans. She was special and wonderful and she couldn't help but be excited to throw it in everyone's face. Turning away from the dizzying beauty of the sun glinting off the strong arms of the tower, she gazed back into the opulence of her room. The satin sheets, the thousand or so pillows, the remnants of the pink champagne they'd celebrated with the night before.

They were always celebrating. Their one week anniversary, their love, their first night in a new country, their last night in a country.

Everything was a celebration to Gerard. Last night he'd been in an especially good mood. He had toasted her over and over and drank the cotton-candy colored champagne out of her hot pink pump. She dropped her head back and laughed aloud at the memory. Silly boy. Where was he? It seemed like she had been sitting here, looking out this window and reminiscing for quite some time now.

Her phone beeped, and she looked down to find yet another text from her mother. Her parents were in a frenzy about the amount of money she'd been spending. She clicked through and found another text from her old roommate, Tess. She hadn't spoken with her since she left her in Prague. She felt a short, violent pang of guilt, which she quickly dismissed. Tess had messaged her to ask if there was any way she would be interested in meeting them for the last leg of their trip in London. She felt another stab of guilt and dropped the phone back to the bed . Quickly, she picked it back up. Flipping back to her mother's text, she saw that in all caps, she had written, "CALL HOME NOW. EMERGENCY". It was strange. It couldn't be a real emergency? Her curiosity got the better of her though. She quickly dialed home, making sure she had the country code. Her mother answered on the first ring. "HELLO? Maggie?! Darling, where's the money? Where is all of your money?!"

She knew immediately what the problem was. With the life they had been enjoying, she

ALEXANDRIA NOLAN

and Gerard had fairly drained her account. She took a deep exasperated breath in, and sighed loudly. She wanted her mother to know how annoyed she was. She calmly explained she had loaned it to a trusted friend, but that it should be back in her account today. "But, Maggie, how could your friend spend that much money? It was a small fortune. Are you in some kind of trouble?" Maggie shook her head, and clicked her tongue on the roof of her mouth. She ran her fingers through her curls, and remembered how ignorant her parents were. Speaking as if to a small child, (since that was probably just about the understanding her mother had of the world) she decided to begin explaining about Gerard and all of the beautiful gifts he had bought her. As she was describing the purses, heels, earrings, watches, pendants and bangles. Her hand danced over her jewelry box, and she was suddenly seized with a feeling not unlike a King in his treasure room, to see and touch all of her delightful accoutrements. But when she opened the lid, it was empty. Her controlled, nasal voice faltered for a minute on the phone.

She feverishly ran over to her train case where she had put some of the other items, but they too, were gone. She grabbed for her wallet —empty. She slowly pulled the phone down from her cheek, and pushed the button to end the call. Her mother's voice could still be heard as her finger found the button. All at once she crumpled into a seated position on what now seemed like an overly large, ridiculous bed. Her lace nightgown seemed insubstantial. She was cold. Cold everywhere. The freshness of the breeze outside, the golden fingers of the sun's rays, even the Eiffel Tower itself, they all seemed to mock her. For, Maggie had realized that not only were her treasures missing, but all of Gerard's things were gone as well. His bags, his shoes, his aftershave. His hair brush, his cologne, his favorite sweater. Gone. Only his musky lavender scent remained.

She picked the note up, once again, and read it. "Do not be angry, mon cher. I have gone. Will you miss me? xx Gerard". It sounded different in her mind this time. A goodbye. She knew then. She knew that she wasn't special. She was just Maggie. She picked the phone back up and calmly asked for the police, all the while knowing he was too good and she was too stupid. Even if they ever recovered her things, she'd never recover all that she'd lost.

"She had always been fond of history, and here
[in Rome] was history in the stones of the street and
the atoms of the sunshine."
—Henry James

3 : ROME

The day was already hot. Tiberius had been up way before the dawn though, preparing himself to attack the day. His equipment was meticulously cleaned, (by his standards at least), and he once again donned the leather strapped sandals, his breastplate and his helmet. He proudly pulled and tugged it, this way and that. It had to look just right. For, Tiberius was a gladiator, and it was as much about showmanship as it was about anything else.

His father before him had been a gladiator, and because of his long, successful career, he had been able to share all of his tricks and strategies with his son. Tiberius had loved his father, but knew that this trade would die with him. For although Tiberius dressed and returned to the great Roman colosseum daily, his gladiator uniform was the only warrior-like thing about him.

He knew what he was. And he could see, that although his son loved him, he was ashamed of him. He may call himself a gladiator, but what was he really? A swindler? A liar? A man who cheated tourists out of their money? He was all of these things.

For a long time, it had been funny. A good joke to play on all of these stupid Americans and English tourists. They would come here to Rome and visit the Colosseum, and as they strolled around the outside of the great marvel of Rome's past, they would find Tiberius! In full regalia! He would walk up to mothers and daughters, lovers, friends, and families and inevitably...they would want a picture! And yes, the picture was free, Tiberius does not charge for pictures. But, after the picture was taken, perhaps a tip? Perhaps a small consideration for providing you with such a remarkable memory of this great, eternal city? Surely, more than a euro. Surely, it is worth more than 5 euros for such a memory, no? Surely, 10 or 20 euros is a more appropriate price to pay for a photo with Tiberius, the last gladiator, yes?

He would see the tension and distress on their faces. He would follow after them, entreating them for his tip. They paid, they always paid. They were afraid not to. For Tiberius might not be a real gladiator, but he was a large Italian man, who seemed very angry. Yes, it had all been fun once. A lark. He used to revel in the discomfort of others, he had swelled with pride at the prospect of emptying euro after euro from these silly traveler's pockets. But that had all changed a few weeks ago. He had finally seen himself through his son Bruno's eyes, and now he felt only shame.

It had been a day like any other. Nothing remarkable at all. It was scorching hot, but he had grown used to standing out in the heat. He felt that it made him more robust, that it made his Italian blood sing in his veins. He had spotted a perfect mark. A middle-aged woman, attractive, who appeared to be alone. He had sauntered up to her, and she had smiled at him. He had made a hand signal that mimicked taking a picture, and she had smiled again, seemingly relieved, or perhaps just happy to be drawn into an encounter, even if it was a wordless one. She had taken a camera out and one of his relatives had been there that day as his "camera man". As soon as the picture was snapped, she uttered an accented "grazie", smiled again and began to leave. But for Tiberius this was his bread and butter, an old song and dance, he knew he could intimidate her into as much as 20 euros. So he began. Cajoling, making his voice run the gamut from caressing to pleading to threatening and right back. He could tell she was terrified and confused. There were so many other men there, all with swindles of their own, none would interrupt him in his game, none would come to her assistance. He could tell his victim was realizing this. She was cursing herself for coming alone, for allowing herself to trust a stranger. The woman turned towards him, her chestnut brown hair streaked here and there with what could have been silver or gold. Her large brown eyes were fearful and she was crying. Not audibly, but tears streamed down her face. He smiled. He knew he had won, but his triumph was short lived.

Approaching him from the side was his son. If the woman was fearful and confused, then Bruno's face was something much worse. Disdainful. Disgusted. He had walked up to his father, shaking his head and had placed his own money into his hand. He had put a comforting hand on the woman's back and apologized to her in English saying that there had been a mistake and she was free to go. She smiled at him and scurried off. Bruno had glared back at Tiberius and spit on the ground, before striding away.

It had wounded him deeply. He had always known that there were many people who did not believe what he did was savory. It had not bothered him in the least. It was his work, he had been brought up to it...it was almost a family tradition! But something in Bruno's eyes. Something in his contempt had bruised him and it ached every time he returned to the memory.

Neither one of them had discussed what had happened at home. Bruno had not said a word to his mother, or any of his siblings, but there was an understanding. A silent understanding that Bruno despised the way that Tiberius made his money, and as much as he respected him as a father, he did not respect him as a man.

What was he to do?

This question had plagued him for days. A growing, gnawing void had settled over him, eating him up from the inside. All of the actions, the words, the lines he had spent his life uttering, shouting...they all seemed empty and weak now. Tiberius felt like a stranger in his own city. Walking down the crowded alleyways, the singsong lilting words of the Italian language he had spoken all of his life, now sounded like nonsense in his ears. The more guttural sounds of tourist's German, French, Dutch or English sounded...sharper somehow. More true. His own language had become a symbol of his lies, his livelihood, a tragic comedy wherein he played the part of the buffoon. He looked back at his life and was proud, but not of his own accomplishments. He was proud of his son, his wife, his family. He was proud of their home and the food on their table. He could not console himself with the feeling he had put it there. He could not bandage his shame with the knowledge that he had provided these things, for he knew that he could have provided them, with probably less difficulty, doing just about anything else.

He walked along, past the designer shops, past a pizza place that no self-respecting Roman frequented. It was still early, and the locals, like him, were out opening the doors to their businesses, setting up their stalls and booths, and preparing for a brief, passing, unremembered day in the city that was eternal, only in that it was eternally the same.

Tiberius was still mulling over the topic that had granted him no rest when he came upon a statue. He was near the Colosseum, and he stopped suddenly and gazed at the figure. It was a man reclined with his right hand resting on his brow. He stared at this hard, stone man. Larger than life. For a moment, he felt his breath catch. He, too had felt this way! He, Tiberius had been larger than life. He had been so sure of himself. His life, his priorities, his beliefs set in the stone of this city. His son had cracked all of that wide open; he had toppled the stone of his personal philosophies. Tiberius shook his head, and gazed sadly at the statue. At once both envious of its certainty, but also shuddering to realize he too had been as immovable.

He continued on. He was almost to the colosseum. He had walked this same path, nearly every single day since he was 12. He had followed this path beside his father, and then alone when he became a man. The same dirt. The same streets. The same earthy, dirty smells of too many people in one place. The same deep, vibrant blue, Roman sky. He looked about him. Something was wrong. Something was different. He could feel it, tickling inside of him. The feeling that something had changed. He stopped. He was on the corner of a street. Streets he had walked down hundreds, thousands of times. More people were out, walking, bustling. He felt himself being jostled by passerby. He lifted his eyes and looked about him. He saw everything as if he was a child, but he knew he had never seen Rome like this, even when he was young. So many people had stood in the spot he was in! So many souls had walked on this street! His eyes rested on the colosseum. He saw it. He was truly seeing it, and it was magnificent. People, *his* people had built that wonder of architecture. He was blessed enough to stand in its shadow every single day. He lived and worked in a city that people all over the world came to visit. A place that many people lived their whole lives to see. He was crying. He realized that wet, hot tears were spilling down his cheeks. He left them to flow, unchecked. Was he going mad? No, his eyes had finally been opened.

He was jostled a few more times. He heard people cursing him for blocking the way in another language. A man shook his fist at him and continued on. He felt another pang of guilt and fear well up inside of him. Fear, upon realization that this anger, this chaos, is what the tourists he intimidated every day had felt. A rushing, searing poke of disappointment to the gut. The visitors had come to his Rome, they had come to visit, to learn, to experience his home and they were treated to threats, and fear of being swindled. He winced inwardly at his own part in this.

Every step had brought him closer to the colosseum. He looked up at it, marveling. He smiled to himself and closed his eyes, trying to picture in his mind the way it looked when it was in its glory. He was proud of his gladiator costume, but for a different reason than he ever had been before. He saw himself for the first time. Of course tourists wanted a picture with him! He was a powerfully built man dressed like a gladiator! They had just gotten done gazing into Rome's past and were looking for a way to become part of it themselves. And he had deceived them. He had turned their love and excitement for Rome and twisted it into a gimmick. A trick. He felt blood again rush to his face, and his head came to rest ashamedly in his hands. How could he fix this? Over 30 years of his life had been spent outside this amphitheater, and he realized he didn't know the first thing about it. He had never even been inside.

His feet seemed to know where he was going before the rest of him had a moment to realize. He was queued up in the line behind the tourists. It was early. The ticket office had barely had time to open yet. It was so important to those lined up with him to see this structure he had taken for granted, that they had gotten in line early before the office even opened. He could hardly believe it. He waited patiently and bought his ticket with the rest of them. He walked in, and up, and around. Everywhere he looked was... unspectacular. It looked almost the same as it did on the outside.

Yet... there was something. Something vitally important about being inside. About his own sandaled feet walking in the same steps as people did thousands of years ago. To walk in a place where real gladiators had fought, struggled, found defeat or victory. Victory to be ogled by rich Roman patricians, or deified by an adoring public. To live one more day until the next fight. The explosion of the crowds. The thunderous rage of their shouts. He remembered from a long-ago lesson in school that the colosseum floor had been flooded for naval battles. He couldn't take his eyes off of it. It wasn't the old ruins that he saw anymore, but an entire city teeming with life and pride. A Rome celebrating its vast reach into the continent, drunk on its own majesty and power. The whole arena came to life with people from all walks of life, to celebrate the glory of an empire that was now long gone, but must have seemed without end. He was moved, moved beyond words, beyond thought. The only thing that seemed to exist for a moment was him and this place. He drank all of this in. He melted into the feeling that he was a part of all of this. He, Tiberius, could still choose to bring that same joy and power to those visiting his Rome.

He spent the whole day inside. He trekked every inch of the grand edifice. He accosted the Italian tour guides and made them feed him more, more, more information. He wanted to know everything. He wanted to understand his colosseum. At first they had seemed confused, but when they found such an eager and demanding listener, they allowed their stories and facts to enrobe him.

That night, as he walked home, he thought of his family. He thought of Bruno and how in his one act of kindness towards a woman he didn't know, he had not only saved her from his father's greed, he had also saved him. He had saved Tiberius from becoming a ruin himself; a solid, unbending, leftover. He had learned so much today. About himself. About Rome. About the colosseum. Tiberius knew, if only one looked at all of these wonders in just the right way, their true significance and power were revealed. He didn't want any longer to be an unhappy memory in a photograph that these visitors would paste into an album, and then cringe at every time they glimpsed the photo.

No, he would be a man Bruno would be proud to have as a father. A man that would enrich a trip to Rome. Tiberius had learned much today, but like a sponge he hoped to soak in much more. He would study, and in the end, work alongside the tourists. He would show them Rome, through his own new eyes.

He was more gladiator in this moment than he had ever been before.

A mind can make a heaven out of hell, or a hell out of heaven. —Costa Rican Proverb

4 : GUANACASTE

Why had she come here? Dahlia felt as though she had been everywhere since her divorce had come through, and it was only now that she could finally pause to gaze backward.

She had started in Budapest. She still wasn't sure how she had taken it into her head to go in the first place. She had simply stomped into the travel agent's office and said she wanted a trip filled with warm countries. She hadn't wanted to use the internet to book anything, mostly because she would have to call her son, Peter, and she hadn't felt like bothering him. He was having relationship issues of his own, planning his own travels...and part of her didn't want to tell anyone.

She just wanted to GO.

Everyone wanted to know why she and Sean had gotten divorced. Of course, it was a natural question. 30 years of marriage and then, suddenly, without a whisper of warning, she had wanted out. No one had seen it coming, least of all Sean. She felt guilty even thinking about it. She knew she had hit him right where it would hurt most, a solid punch to his pride. She didn't like when people asked why it ended, because she didn't have a very good answer. She had never really been herself in the marriage. She wasn't even sure who that was. She had spent so much time trying to be "Sean's perfect wife", that she had completely forgotten to figure out who she wanted to be. She had always been unhappy. Not for any reason in particular, just...she could feel in her bones that something was missing. So much so that the unhappiness had become a part of her. For some women, for some relationships, the easy companionship she had with Sean would have been enough. But not for her any longer. She knew that greater happiness was possible, and it wasn't hinged on another man, it just most certainly wasn't to be found in the life she'd had with Sean.

All the same, it had been difficult. She'd traveled alone, something she never could have imagined doing. She had found her trains, and negotiated with locals, had someone try to pickpocket her in Athens, and a scary encounter with a 'gladiator' in Rome, and along the way had met interesting people. She had traveled from Budapest to Southern Germany, Italy from north to south stopping in Milan, Florence, Rome, Naples, Calabria and then Greece. She had left Greece and had flown here to Costa Rica. She had been away from home for months, and she wasn't sure what she was still looking to find.

The first thing she had noticed here was the heat. It was early December, and this was by far the hottest place she had been. The sun's rays beat down on her exposed flesh. She couldn't imagine heat like this at home in Chicago. It was heat like she had never experienced in her life. It made her want to strip down to her swimsuit and walk around mostly naked all day. If she were still 25, hell, if she was still 35, she would probably do it. But not at her age. She'd lost her confidence.

It was the most startling part about the divorce. It was an awakening. One day, she was living a life that she was unhappy in, but couldn't imagine any other life, and today, she was 52 years old, sweating her makeup off right next to the equator, alone. Change always seems so difficult, so unbearable, but once you've done it, you can't believe you lived any other way. The change becomes a part of you. It was with these thoughts that she sat ruminating, lounging in a chair on the beach, looking out at the smooth, glassiness of the water. Everything seemed still, trapped in time. She felt effortless. Europe had been a dream. The trip, the travels she had longed for all of her life. The love for travel and adventure she had passed on to her son, Peter. She had waited for her turn all of those times he had planned trips and travelled, again and again. This was her time now.

But as busy as she had been in Europe, and anxious and excited...Costa Rica, and this west coast area near the capital city of Liberia, was exactly the next step. The travel agent had planned it all perfectly. Time to reflect. To mourn. To soak in the beauty of the world around her, without having to be in a rush to get anywhere. Her skin looked as brown as a nut, and she was certain that she would have a stinging, crimson burn tomorrow–but she didn't care. As beautiful as it all was, the green, the ever-blooming flowers, the lazy blue water, the tropical scents, the monkeys in the trees, the stately fountains all over the resort; even for all of this, she was in mourning. Divorce is like death. It is the death of a relationship. The death of the version of you that was someone's wife. The death of them as your husband. A part of your character dies, and theirs, but you both must continue living. She knew that she must make herself continue moving forward. For Dahlia though, divorce had also faced her with the fact that she had lost her youth. Her life had flashed by her, and she had nothing to show for it besides her son Peter, who lived out of state and only called occasionally, she had some indifferent "friends" that she had loathed visiting with at the Golf Club on Wednesday evenings, a house she had let Sean keep, and a lot of clothes she didn't like but had thought were appropriate 'for a woman her age'.

Divvying up their possessions had been easy for Dahlia. Sean had broken down and cried as he touched a picture frame, or had come upon a set of candlesticks. She hadn't wanted any of it. Not even most of her own things. She wanted to start over. From scratch. It wasn't just Sean she was leaving, she was leaving the version of herself that had been secretly unhappy for all of these years.

She had gone right across town and rented a one bedroom apartment in a high rise. She had gone to the mall and bought long, flouncy, gypsy skirts and floor-length maxi dresses. She had bought large hats and big sunglasses. She had unrolled her hair from her customary, neat chignon, and let it hang free in long, chestnut waves. She had bought bright coral lipstick, and pointy, heeled boots. She had decorated her apartment in all white and dark brown wood, which Sean would have hated. She had scavenged antique stores, hit up all of the estate sales. She felt like she was 20 years old again, figuring out what 'her style' was. She looked in the mirror and saw someone who had lost their youth, but had still grown younger somehow. She looked in the mirror and saw possibility and relief. And one day, a week after the divorce was final, she looked in the mirror and knew it was time to explore. She had left a week later.

Here she was. In Paradise. She had spent the last three days in the same attitude. Arising with the dawn, eating a small breakfast of fresh tropical fruit and cheese, then bringing a book down to a chaise by the water and reading for most of the day. It was a kind of heaven for her. And then for some reason, on the fourth morning, she awoke with a feeling of needing more. She felt adventurous. She felt as if she had finally awakened after a long sleep from an unfulfilled life. She dressed in cut-off shorts that the "old Dahlia" would have turned up her nose at for being "too short". She asked the concierge if there were any excursions she could sign up for, and preferably for that day. It was unusual on such short notice, he told her, but he was certain he could find something.

After a few minutes of phone calls and rapid fire Spanish, he motioned for her to return to the desk. He had found something, and he seemed very pleased with himself. He was able to get her on the most popular excursion: white water rafting. Her mouth dropped. White water rafting? He couldn't be serious. Her stomach protested by performing roiling somersaults. She asked meekly if there was...anything else? No. That was it.

But she wasn't a 'rafting' kind of woman! She had agreed and paid the deposit, but she felt sick and upset. This wasn't the kind of adventure she'd had in mind. She looked down at her watch and realized, she only had 20 minutes before the bus arrived, and also, that she would need to take off her watch.

When she returned, there was a group of mostly young couples. Some appearing to be honeymooning, and others here in Costa Rica probably practicing conceiving their first child. Her initial reaction was to roll her eyes. But then, she smiled. Some of the young men were Peter's age, and she thought of him and his someday wedding. She hoped he was having a good time, wherever he was right now. She waited patiently in line with the couples, joined now by some other men and women that were around her age. One older couple joined the group and they had their three adult children in tow. It didn't bother her to be the only single woman, which upon realization, felt good. The idea that she was comfortable being alone settled over her like a warm bath. She smiled to herself, proud in the moment.

The bus was comfortable, but the ride seemed an eternity. When one doesn't know where one is headed, the ride is always interminable. She alternated between feelings of anxious dread to impatience with the never-ending ride. They finally arrived and as they exited, she swallowed several times, tasting bile and feeling as if she'd like to run right back onto the bus and hide under the seats until it was all over. The English speaking guide was telling them safety procedures and putting them into pairs. It was six people to each raft, and when she realized she had no partner, her earlier feeling of calm disappeared and was replaced by panic. She didn't mind being alone, but she didn't want it to be commented on, or singled out. She was just about to speak up, when the guide just casually filed her into the boat along with the family with the adult children. They didn't seem to mind her being included, and one of the young men offered to be her seat mate. As they walked along the forest trails, she hardly paid attention to anything. She saw neither the trees, nor the trail, or even where she was stepping.

The moment was surreal. She was nervous for what was to come, and she was relieved at having the problem been solved so easily and without comment. The young man had fallen into step with her, and was talking. She hadn't been paying attention to him, but now realized he was telling her about his family. She noticed he smiled a lot, and easily. She felt a stab in her chest; when was the last time she had seen Peter smile? Had he always been so morose? No. She wished that her own son had the same easy happiness this young man did. She felt her own anxiousness falling away. The young man seemed warm. He introduced himself as Brandon Hartwell, and told her his family had come for his parent's wedding. At the look of confusion on her face, he smiled and said their mother had died of cancer some years ago, and that this was his father's new wife. They had gotten married at the resort yesterday. He called out to his family and turning around had introduced her around, to his father, new stepmother, and his twin siblings Tristan and Tessa. They all offered her a smile and in a moment she felt welcome. She almost wished she had gone on more trips with her family. Would it have helped her and Sean? Probably not. But, perhaps it would have made Peter happier. She felt that same stab in her chest, and wished she had been a little less focused on her unhappy marriage over the years, and a little more focused on Peter.

Brandon looked a little wistful for a moment, and then offered her another smile. She murmured her apologies about his mother, and her congratulations on his father's happiness. He thanked her, and as they walked she told him a quick version of her recent adventures. He seemed genuinely interested, and said that his sister, Tess, had just gotten back from Europe herself. Small world, Dahlia thought to herself. Or perhaps it was because it was such a big world, that instances like that were not that strange.

She felt happier, and lighter nonetheless. As they approached the boats, her reservations had vanished. It was true, she had never been an "adventurous" person before. But, these last months, hadn't she shown herself to be just that? The hot equatorial sun blazed off of the top of the river, a few of its rays catching her eye and fairly blinding her. The jungle they had emerged from had a cool, dark quality that felt both savage and safe at the same time; unsure if the eyes that were watching were hostile or merely curious. She stepped into the white plastic raft, the crisp smell of the tumbling water assailing all of her senses. She was surprised to find that she felt, in her element. She giggled and splashed some of the water that was in the bottom of the raft up at Brandon. He smiled and splashed her back. His family got situated, and the boat in front of them pushed off. A few seconds later, a tour guide jumped into their raft and gave them a few additional directions on how to propel the raft and steer. He then gripped a plastic paddle tightly in his bronzed, expert hands, and yelled "PURA VIDA!" which they all yelled back. It was fellowship. It was an electric, jolting happiness as their raft surged forward into the current.

The sultry air that had encased her since she had gotten off the plane was gone in an instant. Replaced by the refreshing caress of so many windy fingers through her hair and across her face. It enveloped her almost lovingly, so many tiny touches on its journey past her and into the tropical jungle behind them. Brandon nudged her hand and pointed to a monkey hanging above them from a tree. She flushed with pleasure. She took a moment to consider where this quiet calm of happiness was coming from. Surely white water rafting should be more of an adrenaline rush than quiet contentment? Although she couldn't understand it, she simply felt as if she belonged. A part of things. An integral piece of the world around her, as if she had showed up for her life at the precise right time.

The world seemed to race past her. Trees here, trees everywhere, the sound of the rushing water, swirling and glittering, she was entranced by the moment. The guide shouted directions and their paddles would move in time and push them away from rocks that jutted dangerously close, each time a thrilling escape from ruin. Her heart thrummed in her chest, buoyantly beating in time to her paddle strokes.

How long had they been in the water? She had no idea. Between the uncontrollable giggles heaving from the pit of her stomach and radiating through her body, and the permanent grin that was now making her mouth dry, she hardly cared. Dahlia raised her paddle up, and as she brought it back to the bubbling blue, she tumbled out of the raft and into the water. As she fell in, her skin was bitten in a hundred places by the swirling tempest surrounding her. She could hear muffled yells and the furious thump of the paddles. She could not believe the sense of calm that enfolded her. She was not afraid. She hadn't a care in the world. A kind of sweet serenity surged through her, as bubbles floated up through her lungs, and out her mouth. She watched them disappear into the aqua stillness. Her own body felt weightless and her long hair floated about, dancing. Her whole life had been for this moment. She knew she wouldn't die. Not here. In fact, it felt like living for the first time. The rest of her life, flitted and flew past her mind's eye. All of the lingering disappointments, resentments, obstacles and challenges...meaningless. She had been more alive on this day and on this river than she ever had. She smiled, and bringing her hands above her head, she parted the water above her and shot upwards, and suddenly she felt strong arms grab onto hers as they hauled her towards a burst of blinding sunlight.

She was back in the raft, and Brandon was looking at her, concerned. His eyes seemed to search her for something, and when she gave him a smile, his expression relaxed and he smiled back. The guide, still anxious, leaned in and asked her if she was okay. Did she need a doctor? Dahlia's thoughts seemed to fly in her head just as she had so easily glided through the water. She sighed, and looked at him full in the face, whispering "pura vida!"

As she hopped down the stairs of the bus and walked towards the resort, the calm had still not left her. Warm tingles zoomed through her being and she felt awake and ready, asleep no more. She had slept too much already, snoozed through life, always waiting for something to happen. She strode forward in the knowledge that it had happened, and although it didn't change anything in her life, it had changed her. Even though she was still divorced, she was still lost, she was still late to the game, at least now she knew what it had all been for.

At least she finally knew what she was doing here. She was *really* living.

*"Open my heart and you will see
Graved inside of it, "Italy"." — Robert Browning*

ALEXANDRIA NOLAN

5 : AMALFI

The strong yellow arms of the sun reached in through the window of the hotel and held her firmly and snugly. Stella twirled a pen lazily around her fingers and breathed out with an irritable sigh. She clicked out of the room reservation system and looked up. It was only ten in the morning and many of the guests were still lazing over their breakfast— even though it had officially ended a few minutes earlier. Plates with crumbs, and butter knives smudged with Nutella and lipsticked napkins were strewn about the breakfast tables in the blue-tiled hotel lobby.

A myriad of languages were spoken in the little room, and her ears picked up the northern accented Italian that she was used to hearing in Milan or Venice. She heard Spanish, Portuguese, and English in all of its many forms. There were the honeymooners from Texas, a group of girls from Australia and a single middle-aged woman from Scotland, an older couple from Brazil chatted with a young man from Berlin. It was always this way. The whole summer through, from late April to the end of October, people from all over the world would rally to the Amalfi Coast. All of them dreaming with eyes open of the beautiful, impossible place that just seemed normal to Stella. She had lived here or near enough to here for the entirety of her life. And excepting the years she had attended university in Naples, and the sprinkles of trips she had been on, all of her life had been spent within walking distance of this hotel.

It wasn't that she hated Amalfi. No, its charms were irresistible even to her. She fell for its beauty and fantasy qualities as much as the tourists who were seeing it for the first time. She knew she lived in a paradise of color and warmth and dreams. And that was part of the problem. Amalfi was her beautiful, familiar lover. She knew every piece of his geography, every chink in his walls, every twist of his passages. The wide world was her unknown exotic paramour, enticing her with promises of love and excitement that Amalfi could never offer. Where did people that lived in paradise go on vacation? She didn't know.

She had done very little traveling around Europe with her family when she was younger, in most cases too young to recall. She had, however, taken a lone trip to Greece a few years before. She had been so filled with excitement for the history, for the scenery, for the blueness of the water and the bustling villages. She had read the guidebooks and scoured the internet for the restaurants that served authentic food, and the best places to stay. She had waited eagerly for the day of her trip, barely able to contain the excitement she felt at striking off on her own.

But, upon arriving, while the rest of the explorers around her had been in ecstasy over its majesty and loveliness, she had just been reminded of home. The whole country had seemed like a mere shade of the vibrance of Amalfi, and she had found herself on more than one occasion comparing this cove or that grotto to the ones she knew at home so well. It was a curse to come from somewhere that was so irrepressibly lovely. It cast a kind of pall over every other place.

And yet. Yet, she could not help but feel the pull of lands unseen and places undiscovered. Of friends not yet made, and champagne not drunk. Delicacies to be tried and challenges to be attempted. Sometimes the feeling would be so strong that it was difficult to keep herself in her seat. She had the rush, the impulse, the need to move. To go. To burst free one day and leave. She could feel it, a wave out in the sea, making its way surely and powerfully towards the shore...and she knew that when it did come in she would have no choice but to plunge in and allow it to carry her away. Yes, everyone came to the dazzle of the Amalfi coast to vacate their lives, but she needed to *leave* these shores to escape hers. Life is funny that way. One man's escape is another man's prison, a beautiful prison, but a cage nonetheless.

Her phone buzzed on the desk next to her. Bruno, her boyfriend in Rome. They had met at the University in Naples a few years ago, and had maintained an easy, sometimes dramatic relationship ever since. She liked that he wasn't a boy from town. It gave her an excuse to leave and take a train to visit him. She would take the ferry over to Salerno, gazing only for a moment back toward Amalfi, and then direct her eyes straight for the shores of Salerno and the train station. There was always a moment at the ticket counter, where she would feel impelled to buy a ticket somewhere else. Somewhere farther, more exotic. Her eyes would skim over the names of distant places, Barcelona, Paris, Munich, and all the smaller places in between. She'd feel a tingle in her fingertips, an urge to change her plans, but inevitably, her promises to Bruno would prevail. She would arrive in Rome, two hours later, and be greeted by his smiling face.

Bruno loved Rome. He loved Italy. He felt a pride in his home country that was not at all unusual to her in the attitudes of the majority of her countryman. A pride in the Rome of the past, of Italy as the seat of the Empire, the Renaissance, the seat of civilization itself as today's society saw it. But there was so much more world out there, there was so much more to see. Bruno would affectionately take her hand, and swinging it back and forth, would rapidly talk to her about all of the things happening in the city, any news that he hadn't told her over the phone, and of his plans for them during their time together. She would often look at him, and think that as much as she cared for him, as deeply as she felt for him, she couldn't help but feel as if they were on borrowed time. She would look into his dark eyes and tousle his dark hair, and think of what a good husband he would be. What a wonderful father. Just not *her* husband. Not a father for *her* children. It was times like this that she would smile at him and squeeze his hand a little tighter, wondering when their time would be up.

She shook her head quickly, as if clearing the thoughts from it. She typed something sweet but meaningless in reply to his text message, and raised her head to speak to a hotel guest with a question about booking an excursion to Capri.

As a little girl, she had believed that there was nowhere else in the world but this village, there was no other way to live than on terraced hills dripping with lemons and the caressing summer breezes coming off the Mediterranean Sea. She had spent her days splashing at the water's edge and watching the boats cruise around the harbor. Her city had everything, her family, their garden, their cats. What they didn't grow they bought down the twisting alleyways of the Via Lorenzo. The Catholic church and the local school were mere footsteps from her door. Between her grandfather's stories of ancient shipwrecks and the glory of the rowing races between Amalfi and Genoa, Pisa and Venice in his younger days, it seemed that the world was too rich to hold anything but Amalfi.

How quickly the illusions of childhood disappear into a mist of dreams, blown every which way until they can never be pieced back together again. She had grown up, and as she grew older, she became interested in the American pop music she could hear playing from her favorite sandwich shops as she waited for her panuozzo or caprese salads. Her friends ogled pictures of film stars in magazines, and her family went for a month long holiday all over Northern Italy. Her eyes were opened bit by bit by the culture and industry in Milan, Florence, Venice. Why, the Italians up north even looked different than her neighbors back home. Taller, with fairer skin and hair, it was as if she had stumbled into a different land altogether. By the end of the trip she was lost. She had been given a crumb to nibble on, and all she could think of was diving headfirst into the cake.

The strangest thing to her was that her family and her friends didn't seem to have the same need for escape as she did. Bruno would have happily settled down in Rome, raised his family there, and had his descendants continue on in this same way for generations. Her father seemed to find no greater happiness than among the lemons and tomatoes in his garden. He would sear some fish, fresh caught from his boat, and squeeze a chunk of the enormous yellow globe which was the Amalfitana lemon, and the look on his face told her that he couldn't think of a more pleasurable thing in all the world. Not for Stella. It wasn't enough. The simple things in life couldn't satiate her hunger for experiences. Even now, she felt the world spinning, and she wanted to be moving with it, not stagnant, waiting for the "right time".

Hours later, she was dancing down the hotel steps, looking forward to feeling the patter of her soft soled flats on the familiar cobbles of the alleys and twisting vias of the town she knew as well as she knew herself. Every day at work seemed somehow to bring her closer to something, but like the wave, the undertow seemed to draw her a little farther away, too. But, if Stella was anything, she was painfully optimistic that good things were coming. That her ship would come in and her strength would hold. She was off to see Bruno this weekend and the small vacation from the press of familiarity would offer at least a small reprieve.

The rest of the week seemed to alternate between flying and standing still, but by Friday, after her morning at the hotel, she boarded the ferry and made the trip to Salerno. On the ferry she had been pretty sure, but stepping into the train station, she was certain. "One ticket to Madrid, please. No return." She was leaving. It was time.

Stella had a secret though. As much as she dreamed, and as much as she discussed and imagined...she also had planned. She had been planning the escape for years. Cunningly. She had formed relationships with visitors at the hotel. She had researched nanny jobs and places to teach English and Italian abroad. She thought of every skill that she possessed and she plotted and planned how to use them. She had saved money every week since she was 14. She had studied and worked at her poor subjects to get her grades up so that she could win the scholarship to the University of Naples, and instead save her grandparent's and parent's tuition money for her travel plans. Every euro had been deposited into an account. Her parents hadn't known about any of it. Not about the scholarship, nothing about her plots or stratagems. And that was all part of the beauty of it. To truly be free, she had to run away. No expectations, no commitments to anyone. No keeping in touch or calling to check in. She had left a note this morning, somewhere they would find it when she didn't come back. And she wasn't coming back—not until she had seen it all.

She had it all figured out and arranged. A Brazilian family that wanted their children to learn English, a school in China where she could teach for a semester, a wealthy American couple who would pay her to nanny and teach their children to speak Italian. And then all of the places in between. All of the young people that had come to the hotel, including the group of Australian girls who had just left that morning. She had charmed and flattered and seduced scores of people with her kindness, her willingness to be helpful, her single-serving friendship with them at the hotel... and now she would leap frog from one of their lily-pads to the next. From place to place, home to home, visit to visit.

And she did. For two exhilarating years. No responsibilities. Nowhere she had to be, nothing she had to do. Just endless options. From houses that looked like palaces in Beverly Hills, to modest two bedroom bungalows in Excelsior Springs, Missouri. The coast of Vancouver to the coast of Japan. The jungles of Costa Rica and the urban jungles of London, Paris and Tokyo. She had food poisoning several times, she fell in an out of love in almost every place, she met people who she got along with as though she'd known them her whole life, and stayed with people that had seemed much kinder when she met them in Italy. She taught students to speak English, and students who spoke English to speak Italian. She got so drunk she was sick and other times so happy she felt drunk. Every moment felt like an adventure, even the boring moments, the tired moments, the busy days and the days she was exhausted and sore from traveling and exploring; her dreams were realized. She sent a brief but loving postcard from each place back to her parents, knowing it was hardly enough for them, but in the moment she didn't care.

Even as time passed though, there was still an ache. A painful tender spot that couldn't be massaged with travel, that wouldn't be buried in life's pleasures. That familiar lover, stifling yet loving, so comfortable yet too well known to be exciting. Coaxing her, pulling her back towards Amalfi's shores.

She would feel this ache in certain moments. Meaningless on the surface, but played with a chord that resonated long after the moment had passed. She had felt it on her first birthday away in China, and then again looking out on the Pacific Ocean from Hermosa Beach. And then, just a few months shy of the two year anniversary of her initial escape, she found herself teaching two young children in Boston how to conjugate some Italian verbs. They'd been laughing about the word for bee, *ape*, and giggling and teasing one another, and not paying much heed to their lesson. She had been with the family for a month. It was December and the family's house had been dressed up in twinkling lights and bows and greenery to welcome the Christmas season. The children had asked her questions—so many questions!— about her home, her family, her Christmas. She thought she could almost see their brains conjuring up the images she was giving them and comparing them to their own treasure trove Christmases. But in the midst of it all, when she was sure the last thing on a child's mind would be how his tutor spent her Christmas, the young boy said, "Miss Stella, I bet you'll miss your family a whole lot this year. I can't imagine being without my family for Christmas. It wouldn't be a holiday at all." He had smiled at her and fled the room in the way that young children do so well, and it had been the first time her heart had grown cold in her chest. As cold as the fierce Boston December winds blowing outside the window in their little lesson room. Her eyes flitted across the yard in front of her out the window, and she had never in all of the time away, felt so far from her home. From her family, from the security of comfort and familiarity. From lemons and cats and her mother's seafood soup. Her heart squeezed, but then, she willed it to stop. She focused on the life she had built, and letting a long, steady breath out, fogging the window in front of her, she walked away. She knew that the moment hadn't really passed. She could feel the truth of the child's words pressing into her skin, pinpricks on her flesh.

A moment before she had been laughing. A moment before she had been a million miles from Amalfi. But we never know when moments like this are coming. They ride along on the wind and surprise us when the force of them knocks us down, only to continue blowing by, not even noticing the damage they do to us inside.

The truth that whirred around and around in her head, unceasingly, like a song that gets stuck in your mind that you don't even like, but you can't seem to stop playing, was that as sudden as this blow had fallen on her heart, she couldn't call anyone. There was no one that she could reach out to that wouldn't expect an explanation. She saw clearly for the first time, that she had spent the last two years making relationships with places, but not people. She had fallen in love and connected with every new city or port she had been, but hadn't created any real connections with the people there. Sure, she had stayed with them and talked with them and laughed with them. But she had treated the people how travelers usually treat the place. She had wonderful, beautiful memories that were empty.

Shakily she picked up her cell phone, and her fingers punched the numbers. She hadn't dialed them in years now. Two years. But her fingers knew the keys without hesitation. Her father answered on the second ring. "Papa?" she spoke softly into the phone. And without anger or sadness, regret or rage, he asked if she was ready to come home. "Sí". Had the little boy's words really been so insightful? No, but they had cut into the precise right spot. A gaping, raw, sadness that had been gnawing at her for months. Not that she regretted her travels, but she knew now that it was undeniably time to come home.

The flight home had felt strangely freeing. She wondered, not for the first time, if she had placed the constraints of home on herself. Upon landing in Naples, she was surprised to see Bruno waiting in his Fiat. He walked up and kissed her on the cheek, picked up her luggage and carried it to the car. Her surprise continued as their conversation was easy and bright. Her native Italian felt good rolling off her tongue, another caged bird she had locked up for a while. There were no promises between them, no expectations, and she found that she was genuinely enjoying his company. That a hole within her was filling with the light of his smile and the easy tousle of his dark hair. She napped for another hour or so, and then he was waking her up gently, and then half carrying her, half walking her to her door.

The next few days she spent reconnecting with Amalfi. It wasn't tourist season, and so it was quieter. She felt that she was finally alone with her old lover, finally able to have a moment with him away from the prying eyes of the masses. And what did she see? She saw through her new eyes what the place meant to everyone. Until you have been away from Amalfi, she realized, you could never know its beauty. Not really. It captivated, it held you in its thrall. The sultry beauty of this coast was unlike any other place in any other country she had been in. It was remote, yet alive, simple yet filled with complexities and layers. Life was slower but more vibrant, and the moments here could hold the depth of the ocean. She wandered around the fontana in the Piazza dei Dogi, and she ducked into the bakery on the side of the piazza. She had been coming to this bakery all of her life. She had come with her grandfather twice a week, and he would tell her that he had come to the bakery with *his* grandfather. There had been a continuity. A feeling of tradition. The bread was the best bread in town. Many of the restaurants served it to the tourists, but the visitors didn't know that this bakery had been in operation for hundreds of years. That it had kept making bread throughout both wars, that father had handed down the business to son, generation after generation. They didn't know these things. But they still loved Amalfi. And now, she knew she loved it too. She knew its secrets and she was part of them.

All through her travels, her triumphs, her failures, all through her doubts and need for release, it had been here. The symbol of her life, and of her family, and her place in the world. Amalfi may have felt like a gilded cage, but now instead of feeling trapped or stifled she felt comfort. It was a cage for which she held the key. It was a cage to fly from and then back into. To shut herself in or out of at will. She knew she would leave again, but she also knew that she would always come back. That this was her perfect launching pad to lands unknown.

Discovering where she belonged seemed perhaps the biggest adventure she had ever been on.

"Things were a lot simpler in Detroit. I didn't care about anything but boyfriends."
—Madonna Ciccone

6 : DETROIT

Sasha opened her eyes to the blaring red numbers on her clock radio. Her alarm hadn't gone off yet and only the first slinking rays of grey had even begun to intrude on the jet black sleepiness of her bedroom. Why then was she awake?

She realized in her half slumber that there was a warm body next to her on the bed. Too tired to be as afraid as she should have been, she craned her neck around to see who was holding fast to the curve of her waist. One glimpse of the large muscled arm with a crescent moon tattoo on the shoulder, and short cropped copper hair, told her all she needed to know. She turned back around, and rolled her eyes. Brandon. Even as she was rolling her eyes, she couldn't help but sneak a bemused smile. How was it that every time he popped back into her life, she never wanted him less? Always more. Like a growing disease.

She sat up in bed and nudged his arm. Her satin nightclothes felt immediately like nakedness, but at the same time she felt overdressed. She was in trouble. She reached down to the bottom drawer of the nightstand where she knew there were cigarettes stashed. She hadn't had any since she had moved in here two months ago, but she sure needed some now.

Sasha reached over and shut off the alarm. She still had an hour to sleep, but there'd be no sleeping now. She nudged Brandon again, and this time his stormy blue eyes opened right up, and a big white smile flashed, showing off each one of his perfect teeth. She rolled her eyes again, but she also took a little gasp of breath. She had seen those deep aqua pools, dark as midnight, thousands of times, but they always startled her. You could get lost in those eyes. She already had been. She'd been lost in them since high school.

"How'd you get in?"
"Picked the lock." This brought an even bigger smile to his face. He sure was proud of himself.
"That's illegal, you know. How'd you find me?"
"Your Uncle Dan." he pulled the covers back over his body and reached for her waist, pulling her toward him. His arms around her made her stomach erupt in butterflies.

"That's a lie. He would never tell you where I live." His arms left her waist, and soon his fingers were combing gently through her hair. She felt lightheaded.

"Like red waves. I've missed this gorgeous hair and this gorgeous girl." He sat up easily, she could feel his long athletic body resting easily on her pillows. "I told him I had to send you some of your things in the mail. He gave it to me without hesitation." Sasha turned again to see that perfect white smile, at once innocent and provoking. She knew he was telling the truth. If her Uncle had no idea he was coming here, he would have given the address. In many ways this whole thing was her Uncle Dan's fault. She had met Brandon in high school, but they didn't attend the same one. Brandon had gone to the all-boys Detroit Catholic Central, and she'd attended Detroit Country Day. Her own mother, who was in and out of rehab or prison could never have sent her there. It was her bachelor Uncle Dan who believed in her talent, and had thought the right school was her ticket to success. She supposed it would depend on your definition of success. Her needs were few, and through her education at Country Day and then SAIC she had honed enough skill and passion for art and graphic design to get her a job virtually anywhere. Which is what she really wanted. She wanted to be able to go anywhere, whenever she wanted. She had been trapped by Detroit her whole life. She had done some studies in Paris, The Hague, Florence, New York, Portland,

Chile, and New Mexico. She had gone anywhere where things were happening with art. New techniques, artist communities, new exhibitions.

Why had she come back? Something about Detroit's troubles had inspired her. The city was broke. She had heard it was a place that was ripe for women artists and entrepreneurs. She felt drawn to it. Like a sick relative that she had to make a visit to before they passed on, or perhaps became well again. She ran her hand through her thick red hair. It had gotten so long, it fairly fell to the bottom of her ribcage. She was almost done with this city, and she hadn't expected him to find her.

He always found her though. She wouldn't speak to him for months, and he would just turn up on her doorstep or in her bed. Once even kicking one of her boyfriends out. The whole thing was psychotic. Unhealthy. Addictive.

Brandon came from money and had lots of it now. He had been made a partner in his father's law firm just by virtue of his genes. She wasn't sure how often he actually worked. It seemed as if he was always available to track her down and come after her, never allowing her to get over him or let him go. She was so angry with him, and yet needed him. He was a tug in her gut, a wave of emotion. She was a junkie for him. He would float in and out of her life like a gust of warm wind, enveloping her, consuming her, breathing him deep into her lungs, only for him to rip right back out of her life. She had never understood it. By all appearances, he was a stand-up guy; he had been the salutatorian of his class, captain of his wrestling team. He had gone on to law school at Yale, as had every other eldest son in his family, and he now possessed beautiful homes in several places, and automobiles that cost more than several years of rent at any of the places she had lived.

But he had a secret too, and it was her. Some of his friends even thought he was gay. A rumor he did nothing to dispel. He didn't care what anyone thought, and she knew it. He wanted her for himself, and she never knew why she had continued to give in. Perhaps it was how overwhelmingly weak she felt around him. How intense and dramatic their arguments, how passionate their feelings. It scared her. She didn't want to drown in that much emotion.

"I thought you were in Cozumel or Columbia or.."
"Costa Rica." he cut in. Sasha had turned completely around and was now sitting with legs crossed looking right at him. The intensity of her stare seemed to both unnerve and attract him. Her violet eyes blazed, and he leaned forward to kiss her lips. She pulled away, but not quickly enough. The kiss still lingered between them. After all these years, and all of this heartache, how could he still make her feel this way?

"Yes, Costa Rica. So, the old slob got married again? How was it? How are the twins?" Sasha

leaned back languidly, resting on her elbows.
"It was revolting. Poor woman has no idea what she's gotten herself into. He'll probably kill her too" Brandon spat these last words out bitterly. He didn't talk about his mother's cancer often, but she knew that he'd been angry at his father for not doing more. "The twins are fine. They are planning some more European trips. Tessa went this summer and caught the travel bug. Maybe we should join them, eh?" His eyes bored into her with the challenge. Finding she wasn't strong enough to meet his gaze, she turned away.

She shivered. Why was everything between them always so impassioned? Why did it always feel like life or death? They really were like a poison to each other. Experiencing the greatest happiness and the depths of sorrow, running the gamut of emotions constantly. It was exhausting. It was toxic.

Sasha looked back up at him, and was once again struck by how disgustingly alike they were, people had even taken them for brother and sister. In fact, they looked more alike than the twins did. Her friends had teased her about it mercilessly. The thought of that mocking gave her courage, and she spoke the words she had been fighting to say since she had first discovered him in her bed. "I've met someone."

He looked at her strangely, "I meet loads of people."
Losing her nerve for a moment, she couldn't help but ask, "Oh, really? Did you meet anyone in

Costa Rica?" It was a challenge and a coward's way of buying time.

"Yes. In fact I did. I met a very pleasant young man on the plane there, and then I met my father's charming new wife, and I met a wildly attractive older woman whom I had to fish out of the water when she almost drowned." Shaking her head, Sasha replied that she was sure that the woman had shown her gratefulness properly.

"Ah, she did. We became boon companions for the rest of the stay until she had heard so much about you that she urged me to find you immediately. She said, and I quote, 'most people would give all of their appendages for a love like that'".

Sasha's violet eyes turned a shade more purple, and she looked him full in the face. She hadn't thought he had ever talked to anyone about her. She had thought she was a dirty secret, she'd always felt like one. A poisonous, backstreet, gypsy girl who couldn't settle down. "What else did you tell her?"
"I knew that would get your attention. I told her how we met, for one thing." He definitely had her attention, and to drive the point home he cast a fleeting glance at the crescent moon on his shoulder. The shadow moved at the turn of his head, making the moon seem to gleam for a moment, before becoming consumed again in shade. He rose out of bed, kissing the top of her head, and made his way toward the kitchen to start coffee. It infuriated her how cleverly he

found the french press and coffee, and how he remembered to sprinkle cinnamon on top of the grounds, just the way she liked it. He did these things to drive her mad. He did it to punish her, to give her a glimpse of happiness. Turning her mind from these thoughts, she replayed the day they met. Although, she had to admit, she replayed it far more often than she ought.

It had been a charity art show at Country Day. Some of the other private schools had been invited, and the hope was to raise funds for Hurricane Katrina. Sasha had always loved to paint, but usually the art classes didn't give as much artistic freedom as she'd like. But, with the idea of selling these pieces of art to local upper crust families, the school had left students to create without limits. She had produced a haunting painting, entitled "She Awakens by Moonlight". The final product had exploded with longing, desire, wanderlust, represented by a woman gliding off and away on a great black horse, her hair flying behind her, all exposed by the faint light of the crescent moon overhead. She had secretly hoped it wouldn't sell, but because of the imagery and passion that seemed to flow from the piece, it had resonated with nearly everyone who had seen it, and many people had made offers on it already. Until Brandon saw it. He had opened up his wallet on the spot and bought it, and wouldn't take no for an answer. He had then asked to be introduced to the artist, and that's when they had pulled her by the hand to introduce her to Brandon.

The electric charge was immediate. They had locked in on each other, and for Sasha it was like the whole gallery fell away. Forgotten was the uncomfortable black sheath dress a well-meaning friend had lent her. Gone was the boredom of the gawking public. His eyes had burned into her. He had stepped forward to shake her hand, and they had both stopped, still holding hands and looking at each other. It had probably seemed unsettling to those around them. She knew in her heart it wasn't normal, that something was off. His gaze was too needy, she had given herself away too easily. The people around them had moved away, and they were left alone, still face to face. He had done something then that you'd only see in a silly romance novel, or a romantic movie. He'd reached behind her head and pulled the pin from her hair, and watched greedily as it fell down behind her, a flaming red avalanche. "Perfect" he had whispered.

That was the beginning. After that, she would find him waiting outside school for her, or at her house in the morning waiting to drive her to school. He would show up on weekends and drive her to Troy or Rochester. Sometimes in the summer they'd drive all the way up to Mackinac Island or take the train to Chicago. She'd never bothered to tell her mother, because she was either not around, or too high to care–and she had no idea what he had told his family. They had to be together, though. That was all there was.

This same insane need for each other had continued through college. The distance never seemed to bother him. He would show up outside of her apartment in Chicago, or come to her art shows. A plane ticket would arrive in her e-mail for her to come visit him in New Haven, sometimes only six hours or so before the plane was due to leave. He had come several times midweek; she had just walked in with a group of friends to find him making her dinner or napping on her bed. It was crazy. It was a marvelous madness that she loved and hated and couldn't get enough of, but also she couldn't handle anymore. It was a tug of war nightmare of drama and lust and sweetness.

He emerged from the kitchen, giving her yet another of his infectious smiles. And she cleared her throat to repeat, "I've met someone".
His face fell for a split second and then meeting her eyes, "I know. I've heard." Almost as soon as he said those words, he started down a different track of conversation. He asked her how her paintings were selling. Graphic design was her bread and butter, but he knew that she painted in her spare time, and then displayed these works in various galleries, coffee shops or artsy boutiques all around the different cities she had lived in. When one sold she would find her cut of the sale wired into her bank account wherever she was. The truth was, they had been selling very well. She almost couldn't keep up with demand. Some of the gallery and shop owners had even called to say there had been bidding wars between interested parties. She liked the

idea of her paintings all coming to rest somewhere, finding homes, even if her gypsy soul wouldn't allow her the same rest.

She wouldn't be deterred though. "Brandon. His name is Justin. I met him at a graphic design convention downtown near the Ren-Cen. He lives in Houston and contracts with some of the oil companies. I'm moving in with him in a month. We're getting married." While the word "married" still hung in the air, he sat down on the bed and pulled her mouth to his. He kissed her hard and long and deep, and when she came up for air she found that they were both laying on the bed and that she was shaking with desire.

"NO! Not again! You can't do this again!" She sat up and pushed herself away from him. Sometimes she was afraid of him. Afraid of him swallowing her up. How was it so easy to fall right back into their old relationship? Why would he never let her be, yet never stay completely?

"You can't possibly love him. You love me. You only love me. You're mine and I'm yours and there's nothing else." It even sounded dysfunctional. Just hearing the words come out of his mouth made her angry, she belonged to no one. She had worked too hard for what she had, too hard for her degree of success to just give away her soul to Brandon because he expected her to. At the same time, the words were mesmerizing. Like a snake charmer, he knew the exact right notes to play, she could feel the tingles and reverberations of his words playing up and down her body. She wanted to be his.

But, no.

He kissed her again and again. Until she didn't know where he began and she ended. She was wrapped so completely into him and he into her that she felt like she was suffocating, but was horrified to find how much she liked it. She loved being enveloped in him, it was right and wrong and poison and cure all in one. When their lovemaking was over, she felt the same conflicting feelings of shame and contentment that she had come to associate with Brandon. Perhaps he was right, she wouldn't ever know the happiness she had with him with anyone else, but she knew she'd also be sparing herself the pain.

She shook her head as tears began to quickly flow down her face. This had to be it. She couldn't do this anymore. He would never change. This would be her life, being tracked down constantly, like stalked prey, flitting all over the world, every year somewhere new, just to be found again. She needed the stability that Justin offered. She needed a normal life. Even if it wasn't as exciting, she needed something real and true and tangible. Someone who wanted to begin a life with her. She looked over at the crescent moon on his shoulder, and felt his arms around her breasts. He clung to her like a child. His handsome face was filled with contentment and it was clear that he had no idea of the stormy conflict within her.

She brushed away the tears and said his name, he looked up alarmed to see her upset. "This changes nothing. I've made up my mind. You can't ever give me what I need from a man, and I'm not sure I even want you to anymore. We just aren't right for each other. You're a bird and I'm a fish. You're a lion, I'm a mouse. We can't make each other happy without tearing ourselves apart." His face was heartbreaking. A thousand sorrows passed over his pained visage. He brought his eyes back to hers, and as if nothing had happened at all, "I'm taking a shower and then making breakfast".

He stood up and within five minutes was clean, dry and in the kitchen cracking open some eggs. He called out "take a shower and get dressed. I am going to show you something". Sasha felt helpless. She had poured out her plans to him. She had lied and told him she didn't want him. She had made up her mind. He still didn't get it. She sat there crying for a moment, as he walked back into the bedroom and looked at her sadly, skillet in hand. "I hear you, Sasha. I get it. You don't want me. But I have one thing I want to show you before you move down to the swamp, okay?" He gave her a weak smile, and then went back into her minuscule kitchen. She jumped up and ran her fingers through her hair. She had washed it yesterday evening and it still felt and smelled clean. She noticed the unsmoked cigarette sitting on her bedside table and chucked it into the trash. She rinsed herself off in the shower and then threw on an oversized sweater, and pulled some thermal leggings on her curvy frame, all hips and butt and bust. She added some old witchy looking boots she had found among her mother's things. They gave her a closeness to her mother that she had never felt when she was alive, allowing her to imagine a woman who wasn't so dependent on any drug she could get her hands on. A woman that wasn't so hell bent on destroying herself that she shut all those that loved her out. She wouldn't give into addiction like her mother. And that's what Brandon was, addiction and weakness, a death of the soul.

They ate quickly and in silence. She followed him out to his new car. Brandon explained that it was electric. He had flown to California from Costa Rica to pick it up, and had driven it directly here. One glance into the car and she could tell he meant it. All of his luggage was in the backseat. He had literally come right here to see her. For a moment she was touched, but shaking off the creeping feelings of desire, she opened the door and sat down. The drive was eerily silent and neither one of them seemed eager to break the quiet. Finally, though, she gave in. He had reached over to hold her hand and she had snatched it away and asked where they were going. His response took her by surprise.

"I want you to see my house. I can't believe you never have before." Her mouth hung agape. Sasha sat in muddled confusion. Why? Why now? Interrupting her thoughts, Brandon said casually, "You know, he's been in rehab."

"Who? Justin? How do you know that? How would you ever know that?!"

"I have my ways." He smirked and in that moment she was revolted by him. It wasn't enough for him to track her like a vulture, he was digging into Justin's past too?

"Everyone has a history, Brandon. And believe it or not, some people change as they get older. He's a different man now."

"That's what they all say."

"No, dammit. That's what I SAY. " He was so vile. It was so unhealthy the way he invaded her life, and even more unhealthy the way she had always let him. As if her life did belong to him. She was irritated with herself. She sat looking out the window, avoiding those deep blue eyes at all costs. She couldn't weaken, not now.

"I just want you to be safe. I don't want anyone to hurt you. I have to protect you."

White hot anger burned through her skin and left her stomach full of bile. Him? Protect her?! "Brandon, YOU are what I need protecting from! You are the one who hurts me! Can't you just GET OUT OF MY LIFE! I HATE YOU!" She was so full of venom that she felt as if the rage and unfairness of it all had completely overtaken her body. How could he? Had he ever loved her? Was this a game to him? As her anger subsided, she couldn't help but blanche when she saw tears coming down his face. His strong, hard body had collapsed in silent sobs. And so they sat, next to each other, and miles away.

Twenty-five minutes or so later, they pulled up to a beautiful gated community near his father's main law office. He punched in the code and drove in, pulling into a drive at the end of one of the streets. The house was vaguely the same as the others, but alone. It was at the end of the street, and also somehow separate. He turned to her, and wiping his face, said, "You know I have a couple places like this in different cities where the firm operates. I just want to say that they are all the same. You'll see what I mean when you get inside."

Brandon came around to open her door, and gallantly held a hand out to help her up. As she rose to meet his gaze, his eyes were sad, troubled, the tempest inside them wild with darkness. She hesitated for a moment and followed him to the front door. He produced a key from his pocket, and just before putting it in the lock, he stopped. "It makes me so happy to see you here. It's all I've ever wanted to have you here." Sasha wasn't sure how to respond. What was he talking about? What was this about?

They walked in, and her curiosity became bewilderment. She alternated between feelings of appreciation and devotion, to the sickening stab of discomfort. It was her work. Her paintings. Some of them from when she was in college. Every wall, every room. Was this his obsession? What did it mean? Why did he buy all of her work if he didn't want her? Why did he display her art in his homes? He had said that all of his places were like this. Why? Her brain whirred in confusion.

"I bought them all. I tracked them down like I track you down. I have had bidding wars, and I have tracked them to other buyers, and then bought them off their walls. I had to have you. Whatever little bit of you. Sasha, can't you see? How can it be possible that this is where we end? I have spent my whole life, since the moment I met you, keeping you away from my family and friends, and you thought, what? That I was embarrassed? Of you? I was ashamed of *them*. I was ashamed of this life and the shallowness of it. I was ashamed that the only thing impressive about me was that I knew you. With you I could be different, I could be myself. But, you were such a wanderer. I knew I couldn't trap you in a fishbowl. I knew I couldn't clutch you to my chest and hold you there. You had to roam, and I tried to stay away. I waited and waited, hoping you'd call, hoping you'd ask me to come stay. When I couldn't wait anymore I'd track you down and come to you. I knew you had boyfriends, and it killed me. I couldn't look at other women. Oh, I tried. And my father has tried to find me someone, but the electricity wasn't there. It wasn't you. And if it wasn't you, it wasn't anything. I would never have taken your freedom away. If I'd thought you wanted to be tied down, or wanted me for longer, I would have proposed a thousand times! A thousand times a thousand! And you're throwing us away. How was I supposed to know if you never told me? How could I have ever have guessed?!"

Sasha found herself sitting on a sofa. Her head in her hands, a veil of soft flame colored tresses concealing her. What was all of this? Could she have been wrong? Could she have been mistaken about Brandon this whole time? Sobs racked her body. It was more than she ever could have imagined him saying. It was more than she ever could have hoped for. But could she trust it? Was this just part and parcel of their sick, twisted relationship?

He was sitting at the other end of the couch, his eyes searching her form, looking for a chink in her armor. He rolled up his sleeve, "Look at me. LOOK at me. This moon. YOUR crescent moon. 'She Awakens by Moonlight', I had it copied exactly. I wanted a reminder to be that ray of light that awakens you. That frees you from the jail of your mind, and the sordid expectations of the world. I didn't buy all of your art because people didn't want it, in most cases I had to fight people for it, but I couldn't bear to give away any more of you. You're stronger than me. You exist and thrive without me, and I am a shell of a person without you. It is agonizing to hear that you feel 'hunted' every time I track you down. For me it's opposite. It is not a lion stalking his prey and then pouncing on you wherever you've moved on to. Instead, consider it the desperate paddling of a drowning man, and finding you is the first breath of life, finding you is the life preserver. What more can I say? You are right, it is unhealthy. But you are my life. I have known that since we were 17. And in my opinion, it's not addiction that you're scared of, it's love. Love scares you. "

Sasha had stopped crying. She was looking deep into his eyes and seeing him completely for the first time. He was laid out naked before her. The success, the money, it was expected of him. It was a notch on his to-do list. He had grown obsessed with her. But not in the way she had always thought. He was obsessed with her because he loved her. He was obsessed because she had seemed not to need him the same way he needed her. She had put on such a good show of indifference and independence that he had fallen for it. He had accepted her on her terms, when all the while she had been praying that he would ask for more. But he hadn't, because he thought she was happy. And never having a choice in his own life, he had given her all of her own choices. Her heart swelled in her chest, and she swallowed a sob. This strong, confident, beautiful man loved her. But both of them had been too scared to say anything, too cautious they would lose one another completely by demanding something from the other.

She couldn't process it. It was a dream, it was a nightmare. It had always been so raw and real and consuming. But he was right, she was scared of love. She was still scared he would swallow her, that he would burn her up. She did the only thing she knew. She ran. Out of the house, into his car, and pulled away alone into the morning air. She bolted into her apartment, feverishly packed a suitcase, and was waiting at her gate at the airport within an hour. She sent a text to Justin. "Something came up, I'm coming early. Pick me up at 4 from Hobby Airport. xx"

"In these days of difficulty, we Americans everywhere must and shall choose the path of social justice..., the path of faith, the path of hope, and the path of love toward our fellow man."
—*Franklin D. Roosevelt*

7 : WASHINGTON D.C.

The nervous excitement in the air was palpable. It ran like a fever from the flutter of the hearts and the tapping of the feet of every student in Mrs. Keel's 6th period class. A kind of electric current that ran across the desks and through shoelaces, through the ends of the hair of the adolescents and through the end of their pencils onto the paper in front of them. They were all listening... of course they were. Mrs. Keel was a young and popular teacher. She was funny and didn't take things too seriously, but today there was something else on their minds. They were listening, but not *really* attending to her most excellent discussion on the character flaws of that celebrated Dane, Hamlet.

No, they were already miles away. It was Friday, and it was the Friday before Spring Break. Many of the students would be leaving together after school to go on a class sponsored trip to Chicago, the more affluent students would be tripping down to Cancun, Panama City or the Dominican Republic. But for Josie, in her mind, she was going somewhere much better. She was going to Washington D.C., with Tyler.

Honestly, she was interested in D.C. because she loved History and all that, but... she was most excited about a week with him. A week away from her parents, and instead she got to spend time with her favorite person in the world, the only person who really understood her, her wonderful, fun-loving, always smiling... brother.

She looked up and realized the minute hand was making its last revolution around the face of the clock. She could feel the intake of breath, the tension of 30 other expectant teenagers around her waiting to bolt out into a week of freedom, and she smiled. He was swinging by to pick her up after class, and he would already have her bag in the car. They would drive directly to the airport and then in a few hours, be blissfully far away from her dreary life here.

As the bell rang she looked around and saw flashes of pleasure and release on each of her classmates faces, they had all been packed up for the last five minutes, and looked ready to pounce, looking anxiously at Mrs. Keel, waiting for her permission to stampede out the classroom door. She gave a slight nod, and Spring Break had officially begun. Josie waited at her desk until everyone had made their escape, not wanting to be tossed around or jostled. She was the kind of person no one ever noticed unless she was in the way, and she didn't feel like starting off her break with hurt feelings. She stood and peeked out the second floor window of the classroom, and thought she could make out her brother's truck in the parking lot. She skipped toward the door and waved a fond goodbye to Mrs. Keel, and her own adventure began.

Josie slid easily into the seat next to her brother and was instantly under the spell of his smile. He always immediately elevated her mood. The slow melodies of Billie Holiday washed over her and she could feel the corners of her mouth lifting slightly already. Tyler had introduced her to this jazzy feel-good music on their last trip, and now upon hearing it, she was swept away with the easygoing possibilities that always seemed to be within reach when she was with him. She ran her hands through her curly, blonde hair and pulled it quickly into a topknot. She popped her legs underneath her in the seat and turned toward him. He was beaming. "You ready, sweet girl?"

She was. She pulled her sweater down over her stomach and stared down at how big her legs looked on the seat. Nope. She wasn't going to care about anything this week. Not her weight, or her math grade or her parents. Nothing.

The plane shuddered down on the runway, causing Josie to come out of her reading trance. She had gotten so caught up in the book she had fairly forgotten where she was. She felt a squeeze on her arm, and looked over to see Tyler sleepily smiling at her. He always claimed he couldn't sleep on planes, but here he was, once again, happily awaking from a slumber. She shook her head and gave him a soft punch on the arm. "Loser!" He grinned at her again, crazily, and they both started laughing. Tyler was always a breath of fresh air, and a relief from the seriousness of her home life.

He hadn't always been. And they hadn't always been so close. There was the age difference for one thing, and then...the tragedy. He had been different after that. Her parents didn't think she knew or understood what had happened, but she did. Kids are never as oblivious to the chaos that surrounds their lives, no matter how much parents seek to hide it from them. She hadn't understood all the details at the time, but, as the years had gone by she had collected and pieced together more and more of the story. His girlfriend, Miranda, had committed suicide, and it had changed him. Of course there was more to it than that, but, that was the part that affected her. He had changed, and the rest of the world might mistake him for a bumbling, grinning idiot, but not Josie. She knew those who saw him that way were not really looking. Pain has many faces, and his was a clown's.

She liked traveling with Tyler because he planned trips differently than their parents did. He just had a vague outline of places to go and things to do, and so the whole trip just felt like a spontaneous string of encounters with all of the things she most wanted to see. Traveling with her mother and father, on the other hand, always felt like a regimented military-style operation. Now, being away from them, she almost felt like breathing itself came easier. They had checked into their hotel, had dinner and slept, and now were up ready to explore the city. Tyler was really into American History and politics, and knew practically everything about it. He had an anecdote for every sight and historical facts about the construction and use of all of the memorials, statues and buildings. In all of the photos they captured, in front of the White House, posing with Lincoln's monument, outside of the Smithsonian, the siblings looked half crazed and half drunk. Tyler had this way of fake laughing before every snap to give himself a more "natural smile", but it really just sent them both into fits and made their pictures look absolutely ridiculous. Which was fine by Josie, it felt like it had been a long time since she had laughed.

He had made reservations that night at Tosca, which hardly surprised Josie; she was used to his displays of affection for his little sister. It still meant the world to her though. At home, she was nobody special to anyone, but with Tyler...it was like she was a completely different person. They talked easily of their favorite sights from the day, for him it had been the Smithsonian Air and Space Museum and the Wright Brother's plane inside, and for her, surprisingly, it had been the Vietnam War Memorial. She had been especially touched by that seemingly never-ending wall of names, and had been caught off guard by how strongly it had affected her. It wasn't a period of history she was particularly interested in, but the sheer number of names and the stillness of the moments while they had been there, had felt like a shroud pulling over her. So young, so full of life, men right about her own age, or Tyler's age. Men with *real* reason to be frightened, angry or alone, and despite these feelings, if they did in fact have them, they had died bravely, for their country. It wasn't about her, but it was. It was about life, and war, and time. It had left her with a dull ache in her breast, a darkness that she couldn't illuminate for the rest of the day. Tyler of course, noticed her distress, and had been doing his utmost to make her laugh, or to make a fool out of himself. As much as she appreciated his goofiness and desire to brighten her mood, she still wasn't able to clear the storm clouds in her mind by dinner.

"What exactly has you down, Jo-Jo?" Tyler's face had lost its moronic smile.
"I don't know, Ty. Just something about that wall

on the memorial. It just felt so...finished. The deaths were so...final. Y'know? Just seeing all the names like that, it just got me thinking, I guess."

"Thinking about what, exactly?" He had leaned forward, all of his attention on her. He was good at that. Putting the needs and worries of others first and foremost in his mind. "Something wrong at school? Or with Mom and Dad? Do you need to talk about anything?" Sometimes it was maddening to her how he knew exactly what she wanted to hear. Sometimes she almost hated it. She didn't want to think about her problems. She wanted to pretend, just for this week, that she wasn't unhappy. She wanted to pretend that she was popular and well-liked. She wanted to pretend that she wasn't struggling in some of her classes and that her parents didn't say things that made her want to fall into a hole and be swallowed up. She wanted to pretend that there was no confusion in her heart about boys or girls or who she was or where she was going. But, of course these things couldn't be pretended away. And Tyler had far too many of his own demons to be blinded to those that swirled around her.

She guessed that he probably already knew most of it. But she also knew that he was the only one who wouldn't downplay her unhappiness, or trivialize it in any way. She reached across the table, trying not to look at what she thought were her revoltingly large arms, and grasped his hand. It was warm, like his heart, like his kindness, and her own worries melted into a thousand words.

"It's everything. It's Mom and her constant nagging about my weight. I mean, I know I'm chubby. I know I should eat less, workout more, whatever. But she just makes me feel so much... worse. I know she doesn't mean it unkindly, but, it's my body. I know what it looks like, y'know? God, Tyler. I miss you. I wish you were still at home. You have no idea how much I have been looking forward to this trip. Sometimes I feel like you're the only person in this world that wants to be around me. The kids at school treat me like I'm not even there. Teasing would be an *improvement*, I mean, at least then I would know they see me. But, I don't matter. My grades aren't the highest or the lowest, I'm not obese or shapely, I'm not ugly and I'm not pretty. I'm just...ordinary. NOBODY is interested in me, and when I look in the mirror, I don't even wonder why. *I'm* not even interested in me. I'm just this colossal waste of space, and one day I'll die and my name won't end up on a wall for being brave, and no one will probably even notice." She paused and took in a large gulp of air, drowning on the string of her own words. "Sorry, that was all pretty dramatic, right?"

Tyler leaned in further and offered Josie a small smile. He squeezed her hand, and tilted his head, as if he was really reading her; looking into her soul. "I don't think it's dramatic. Life feels very urgent sometimes, right?" His clear eyes and blonde hair mirrored her own. But where she felt she was plain, he had an easygoing handsomeness. She frowned and looked down into her lap. Josie was realizing that the thing that she most had wanted to get away from was herself...and there was no vacation for that.

"Listen, Jo. A lot of things feel wrong right now. That's life sometimes. Just...wait. Wait. High school will be over before you know it. You will probably never see any of these people again after this June. And getting high or low grades doesn't determine your intelligence. Maybe you just haven't found *your thing* yet, right? Wait for it. You *will* find it. The world is so big, Jo. SO BIG. There are so many other places, and people, and things to get passionate about. No one cares about your weight, you look beautiful. I'm glad you're not stick thin, it tells me that you enjoy yourself. That you eat the things you like. That you aren't spending all of your teenage years dieting and running and trying to look good for people that you won't see again as soon as you walk across that stage. Just enjoy it, kid. It's okay if you don't have it all figured out. You're lightyears closer than I was at your age. I'm proud of you, Josie-girl."

Tyler gave her hand a squeeze and leaned back into his chair. He always knew the right thing to say. It hadn't fixed anything...no words ever fix anything when there's a hurt on your heart, but it felt good. It gave her hope. During the rest of the meal they talked and laughed and dragged up memories from their weird too-old-to-be-at-Disney-World-trip from last year. As they walked out, full of good food, good memories and good conversation, Josie felt her heart swell. She had smiled more today than she had in months.

"Thanks, Tyler. For all of this. Seriously. I don't know exactly what happened to you to make you into this kind of brother, but I'm glad. I can't imagine how I'd get by without your pep talks." Her voice had taken on a faraway quality, and her eyes were two pools of secret sadness.

"What do you mean? 'Get by'? That sounds a little serious, sis."

"Well.. I mean, you know. It's stupid."

"It doesn't sound stupid. It sounds like something you need to tell me right now." His voice had gone strangely tight, as if he anticipated her confession. She hadn't heard his voice like that in years. It was the old, uncaring, angry Tyler's voice. It scared her. She looked up into his face and saw fear. He was afraid of what she was going to tell him.

The last stripes of day had long since faded into darkness there in the capital. To an observer they probably looked like a strange couple. A tall, blonde, Viking-looking boy with a lopsided smile and a face that shouted mirth, but was at the moment constrained into cold marble, and a shy, blonde cherub of a girl with baby-fat on her cheeks and a flouncy tulle skirt. The air between them had crystallized though, no longer the easy flow of conversation it had been. The D.C. skyline offered a backdrop that only further seemed to add an element of seriousness to their discussion.

"Ok, well, a few months ago, I took some pills. It was no big deal. I took some activated charcoal like ten minutes later and threw it all up. No one knows. It was lame, ok? I know that. I just, felt helpless. Sometimes I feel like everyone's life would be easier if I wasn't around. Like, I'm not really adding anything worthwhile to anyone else's existence. I'm just another kid for Mom and Dad to dress and feed. My teachers wouldn't even notice if I was absent...I don't have any *real* friends, Tyler! Do you know what that's like? I'm nothing. I'm worth nothing, I can offer nothing, I have no one." The words were coming out so fast that she hardly noticed that she was practically choking on her own tears. He was holding fast to her, his face expressionless. She had collapsed into her own sobs and as they shuddered through her body, she was repeating something unintelligible about not being very good at pretending. He held her close and let her cry. In his experience, getting the tears out, sometimes until your head throbbed, really was the best way to feel better. When the torrent seemed to have tempered into a drizzle, he sat her down on the first bench they came to and stared into her face.

Josie was smart. He knew that. She was pretty too. Maybe not a classic beauty, but she was pretty in the way you'd want your daughter to be pretty. Wholesome, sweet, angelic, her soft blonde, almost-white hair that spiraled every which way. How had he missed the signs? He figured she was unhappy, typically teenagers were, in one way or another, but he had no idea how isolated she felt. He remembered the feelings himself, how deeply isolation penetrates — how easily it can trick you into thinking that nothing about you matters.

"Jo, I look forward to our trips too. You're my little sister... and, I feel like I can put my guard down around you..."He stopped mid-thought. How could he explain to her the agony of every day since Miranda's death? How could he explain that he knew exactly how she felt? How could he explain that his own path had taken him through the same shaky suicide attempts, the same feelings of worthlessness, the same desolation and sorrow? What were the words he could say? He grasped for them, blindly in the dark, waving the arms of his mind frantically to locate the magic words...but there were none.

He looked out into the darkness, her eyes were glued to him, expecting him to make everything better. Waiting for him to throw her a rope, something to hold on to for another day. His eyes fell on all of the stark white buildings of the capital. And, suddenly he filled with hope. In himself. In Josie. In the world. All of the memorials in this place, all of the museums, all of the decisions being made here daily that affected everyone in this country. There had been struggles on this soil for hundreds of years and there was fear in everyone's heart. There was doubt here, but there was also hope. People had fought and died and given their lives to making this the kind of place where people could sit on a park bench and feel hopeless. Their heartbreak was a luxury and a gift. If you're heart is breaking, it means you're breathing. You're living to endure the pain. A hundred thousand heartbreaks were happening all around, and a hundred thousand more were still to break. It was beautiful. And suddenly he knew exactly what to say.

"Josie-girl, listen, the obstacles will never stop. Life will never get easier, only harder. This is the youngest we will ever be, and every moment after this we will look back on tonight and laugh about the things we thought were hardships. Every moment is a birth, and we can indulge our sorrows, or we can smile through them. I have forced myself into feeling joy every day since Miranda died, and I will continue to do so. And so will you. There will always be something to cry about, but there's always a million beautiful reasons to smile. So, choose that. That's all I can say. I wish I had something more poetic, but I don't. Choose beauty. Choose love. Be unbelievably thrilled with every moment you are able to meet. You will never meet the same one again."

He sat back against the bench as the night around them deepened. He heard Josie take a sharp breath in, and when he looked over she was slumped down into the bench, her skirt encircling her, almost protective, and her face was revealed in the soft glow of the starlight. When she finally spoke, her voice was calmer, and filled with a new confidence.

"You're right. And for the next few minutes, I choose moonbeams and freedom and navy blue nights with a pretty incredible big brother... who is just as messed up as the rest of us, but is better at hiding it." She winked at him, and he smiled. His eyes traveled up to the same sky, in the epicenter of the free-world, and he added, "That's the key, Jo. Sometimes you cover it up so well, you forget where you've hidden it."

As they walked back down F St. towards 10th St. and Ford's theater, Josie knew on the outside nothing was different. She was still chubby and plain, but it was up to her whether she was forgettable or not. She had six days to soak up a beautiful vacation with Tyler, to learn about the past, to think about what she wanted for her own future. Perhaps, Monday when she returned to school she still would feel alone, but, maybe she wouldn't. Maybe she should stand up in the crowd of kids and allow herself to be jostled about, maybe she should risk the rejection of some in order to make connections with a few, maybe she should smile through the pain of taunts and fear of exclusion. After all, she thought while linking her arm in Tyler's, sometimes the best thing to do when life crashes into you, is to nudge it right back.

"You all may go to Hell, and I will go to Texas"
—Davy Crockett

8 : HOUSTON

He took a deep breath in, and coughed. Dan didn't like the city. His ears seemed to ring continuously with the sounds of squealing brakes, the constant thrum of construction and the roar of a far off motor cycle. The air felt dirty. He'd been a lot of places, camped, hunted, seen his share of the world, but he didn't get why anyone would choose to live in a swarming, swampy, stinking city. He walked out of his hotel, and looked up at the jagged knives of buildings that seemed to be grazing the sky itself. He thought of the view from his own property out in west Texas. The air seemed brighter at home. The morning clearer, and night time was darker. The inky darkness would swallow you whole after the sun went down.

Sounds were so clear that nature felt as if it was in the room with him, instead of safely outside his bolted doors. On some nights, the silence was so absolute, his own rustling around in bed, and the sound of his own breath startled him. No, that kind of thing had no place in this city. Only two women could ever have brought him into a city, dragged him from the refuge of the comfort of his home, and one of them was dead and buried.

He always felt a surge of warmth when he was about to see Sasha. His girl. She seemed to feel comfortable just about anywhere she landed, and so she was flying and flitting about continually, never settling down. He was just happy that she had landed here for a spell. The valet brought out his dusty old truck, and after giving him a tip, Dan hopped into the driver's seat. He turned to the backseat to deposit the packages. He wasn't sure about either of them. The weight of them seemed to stay in his arms, even after he had laid them down carefully on the seats. She was down here to settle with a new boyfriend, did she need to see either of these secrets? If he knew they would make her happy he would lay them at her feet the moment he saw her, but, he didn't know. Which would cause happiness? Which pain? Or would they both hurt her?

Dan considered himself a simple man. He had always lived out in the country, a good 45 minutes or so from the closest town in west Texas, except for a brief miserable stint in Dallas when he earned his degree in Mortuary Science. His family owned the funeral home in town, and he had grown up knowing he would be an embalmer. His brothers were in charge of running the home, presiding over funeral services, and interacting with the families. That was exactly how Dan had liked it. When he got back out on his land he lived peaceably, and was known around the area as the man to call if you needed some minor plumbing or construction fix. Or if a rattler had gotten up on your porch, or under your house, or even in your home, it was common knowledge that Dan was the man to call. It was routine, but the bobcats in his yard and the coyotes that he would hear outside, along with those rattlesnakes, kept things interesting.

Life here in the city though, was too much for him. He had only gotten here last night and he was ready to turn his truck back onto I-10, tuck tail and get back to his life. The stress of the situation alone was enough to drive him crazy. Could he do it? Did she even need to know? Would it do her any good? He glanced back at the packages again in the rearview mirror, and caught a glimpse of his own shoulder length blonde hair, lined tan face and icy blue eyes. Sort of a rough and tumble Fabio of the wilderness. The thought made him laugh, but before the sound came out of his mouth, those two damn packages caught his eye, and his worries returned.

He sat down at the little restaurant with his coffee. He felt violated somehow that he had just paid five dollars for a cup of coffee made by a snotty kid. He positioned himself in a table facing the window, so that he could see when Sasha was coming. His eyes stole over to his truck again, and the contents of those packages made his stomach somersault for a moment. Everything fell away when he saw the unruly flames of her hair bobbing up and down from a round bursting knot on the top of her head. She walked in and her violet eyes lit up. He stood up, in the thrall of those dangerous eyes. Her mother's eyes. He shook his head quickly to clear it, as she ran towards him and disappeared into his open arms. She smelled like lemons, which was just one more thing that reminded him of Cora.

"Hey baby girl, how ya been?"
Dan pushed her coffee closer to her, he had made sure to make it exactly like she liked it, cinnamon and all. She slid into the seat across from him, and though her face was lit up, she looked strained, as if it was taking all of her effort to keep the smile in that spot.

"Thanks so much, Uncle Dan. Driving all the way out here...helping me get settled...thanks."
Her eyes flicked upwards, and it caught him off guard. Those eyes always did.
"Darlin', I'd drive all the way out anywhere for you. Don't you forget it."

She looked at him quizzically, and her face seemed to ask a question. But instead she said, "It must seem crazy to you. Me moving in with some guy I met. But really, thanks, it's so great to see you."

"Sasha, nothing you do ever seems crazy to me, and everything you do seems crazy to me. It doesn't matter, though, you're a grown woman whose been making her own decisions for quite a while, and it looks like they were all good ones. I wouldn't have you any other way, baby girl."

Her smile lit up the room, or at least it seemed that way to Dan. A genuine one. But when he asked where her new boyfriend was, it disappeared like the sun behind a cloud. "He had to work in the morning, but he's getting out at noon so that we can all get me moved in." A cloud passed over her face again, and a faraway look came into her eyes. Dan himself was focused on the door of his pickup. He had his confirmation, she wasn't happy. But which package? Which secret? His eyes traveled to the street in front of the shop, and his eyes only met with the gloomy grey of the street, the continuous stream of cars that made up the landscape in front of him. How could a place like this, so devoid of color, so full of the stain of monotony, inspire someone as talented as his Sasha? His mind floated back to Cora, and it surprised him how little he still thought of her unless he was faced with Sasha. She had been just as entranced with new places, but she had been nowhere near as talented as her daughter. She could play a few instruments fairly well, but between the storm of black hair and those violet eyes you couldn't hardly hear the music anyway. He had met her at a honkytonk in San Angelo and had even gotten her to stay with him for three months, until the road called to her again. He hadn't heard from her again for six years. She'd confessed everything when he'd visited her at the rehab in Detroit, but made him promise not to repeat any of it unless she couldn't get herself clean. But she had. And in the end it wasn't the drugs that got her, but that too was a secret.

So many secrets. They say that honesty is the best policy, and that the "truth shall set you free", but it wasn't he who deserved to be set free, it was Sasha. And he just didn't know which truths would do that. It was the not knowing that had been eating him up inside for the last two days.

He reached across the table and grabbed her hand, and she smiled up at him. "How do you like it here?"

"It's a place. Like any other. There are some interesting things going on in the artist community here, and some of the city beautification projects are quite lovely. But, I don't know. It's a place."

"Why'd your plans switch so quick, chickadee? Thought that you weren't supposed to be moving down here for another few weeks?" As he asked, he saw her wince, but he knew it was the right question. She sat still for a moment, gazing around the coffee shop. The barista had made a heart in the foam of her coffee, and she stared down at it for a moment. Dan could hear about a dozen different accents around him, engaged in just as many different conversations. The grind of the coffee machine. How does one tell another person, 'I'm your father'? How does a person admit that they've been lying to you your whole life because your mother asked them to? These moments always seem to happen at the most ordinary places. Maybe it was because life itself was ordinary, and the dramas it held really weren't as destiny-altering as they felt at the time.

Finally she looked back up at him, tucking a stray flaming tendril back into the knot.
"Well, plans changed. They changed because, well, because...because Brandon came up to see me." A look of agonizing sadness passed over her face and then was gone like it had never been there. He knew not to press. That boy had been around throwing things into confusion for years. She wouldn't say anymore than that, and he didn't ask. He knew enough. He found his gaze resting again on the back seat of his truck in the parking lot. How much more dysfunction did his girl need?

She asked about his house out in the country, and he decided to stall it all, and tell her a story. Maybe they could both forget the troubles plaguing them, even for just a moment. "The night was so dark that it felt like my body had been bathed in shadows, I had heard the yowl loud and clear from my bed. I could tell it was a big cat, and that she was in trouble. I grabbed my bowie knife, and a flashlight, threw on my Carhart coveralls and some rubber boots, and I headed out. The stars were bigger and brighter than you've ever seen. Like sapphires gleaming in the night, and they seemed so close that I could practically have plucked them straight out of the sky and made you a crown out of them. It was so dark I couldn't see my feet below me, or my hand in front of me, except when I stood in the starlight at just the right angle. I followed the sound of the desperate crying of the cat. It had sounded closer, but I soon found myself pushing past prickly bushes, and nearly tripping over the knobby roots of the mesquite tree, past waxy leaves, through the crunch of the dry dirt and grass, and to the bottom of a pecan tree. The bobcat was laying there, and didn't even move when I crouched down."

Dan knew that Sasha loved stories about animals, she always had, even when she was little. He would tell her stories of runaway horses and silly coyotes, cunning rattlesnakes and terrifying copperheads. He could almost see her painting the picture in her mind as he was speaking, as that was precisely what she had done with his other stories, painted them again and again. She loved most to paint about nature, and she always said there was nothing purer to paint, and nothing filled with more mystery and longing. The way she painted it, he almost felt like he was reliving the moment himself, but this time with greater intensity. He had managed to purchase a few pieces of her work, and the detail and haunting beauty of them stopped him every time. Just like her eyes did. Cora's eyes.

"The cat's paw was a mangled mess. So I picked her up, and I think she was just as surprised as I was that she didn't bite me. I brought her to the back porch, and went in for some antiseptic and an old cotton t-shirt. I poured the peroxide on her paw, and she hollered like all get-out. I just looked right into those big yellow eyes though, and I think we understood each other. I tore the t-shirt into shreds and bound the paw up. I brought some lunch meat outside, and a bowl of water, and made sure the dogs were locked up tight in their kennel. She seemed comfortable out there, and so when I was done I went back inside and got into bed. Just like it was any other night. Things don't seem so strange if you pretend to yourself that it's normal, and so I did. I pretended it was an everyday thing for me to carry around wild cats in my backyard that could scratch my face right off my skull. I flopped right into bed and slept hard, high on adrenaline. When I woke up the next morning, the bobcat was gone. The lunch meat was eaten, and a few weeks later I found the white cotton shreds in the woods as I walked the property. I haven't seen that cat since, but I felt good about it. When she needed me, I was there, and she let me help, and off she went again in the morning, to live her own life, free in the wild."

As Dan finished his story, he saw a smile going from ear to ear on Sasha's face. The story wasn't completely true. He had seen the cat since, she had come and eaten one of his chickens, but the message of the story was as important as the story itself. She had to know that he admired her independence.

"That was a great story, Dan. You know I'm going to use it for one of my paintings. What a great visual of the cat sneaking off in the early morning light, without even a backward glance for her rescuer. Powerful stuff." She sat back and looked at her watch. "It's eleven o'clock, Justin will be out of work soon. I guess, then, we'll be moving me in." She said it almost as a sigh, and Dan felt a stab in his heart. His blue eyes almost pierced through the doors of his truck. He could see both packages perfectly in his mind's eye, and somehow, he knew exactly which one she needed.

"Baby girl, you stay right here. I got something for you in my truck." Her face looked surprised for a minute, and then she cried out sweetly, "UNCLE DAN! No! Don't you dare give me anything, after all that you've done for me all these years! After driving all the way out here and paying for a hotel? No sir!" Her violet eyes danced all the same though, and it was confirmation that she needed to see what was in that package.

As he stood up, she asked, "By the way, where are you staying? I'd be more than happy to pay for it, seriously. I'm a big girl, ya know." The same look of mischief was on her face, and he was glad that the sadness hadn't had time to return. "I'm staying at the Icon, in downtown. And, don't worry about paying for it, they set me up nice with a suite." With that, he walked out the door to his truck, and if he had turned around he would have seen her shaking her head in disbelief.

His feet felt heavy as he walked towards the truck. The same truck he drove into town every week to prepare the bodies. The same truck he packed up with his rifles and tents when he went hunting. The same truck that he used to help his neighbors with snake problems, or to fix a broken sink. It had never held anything more precious or more important than the two secrets in his backseat. They both had been wrapped in brown paper, and he brushed his hand over them. What did she need to know? Which one of these truths would lead her to happiness and a greater certainty of her worth? This was a little girl who had known nothing but secrets, dysfunction and sadness, but also hope. He had seen that hope illuminated out of her six year old face, he had seen that same resilience of spirit in each of her paintings. And his hand came to rest on one of the packages. This was the one. This package held the secret she most needed. His steps felt lighter as he headed back towards the door of the coffee shop, clutching the package to his chest like a life preserver. Before he reached the door though, he turned around one last time to look at the skyline in the distance. Just that morning he had been amongst those shards of glass that reached desperately towards the clouds. Maybe that's what it was here in the city, a constant grab upwards for everyone. Reaching, reaching for God knows what, and the possibility of one day catching hold of it. There was less mystery in the city, and it seemed more bleak in many ways... but perhaps there was more hope in a place that was teeming with people's dreams. Perhaps that's why they all lived right on top of one another, breathing each other's air, and blocking out the deafening sounds of the city by wearing equally deafening earbuds in their ears as they ran on relentlessly on this never ending treadmill. He would never understand it, and as he turned back to the door handle, he felt a tug in his chest, a feeling that hastened him towards delivering this package and getting this moment over with, so that he could return home to his refuge of absolute darkness and complete bright light. Where there was no confusion, or middle ground–just nature.

He stepped in and sat down, handing her the package all in one movement. "Uncle Dan, you seriously didn't need to get me anything."
"Chickadee, it's not from me. It's supposed to be something for your new place."
"What do you mean, 'not from you'? Who's it

from?"
"Just open it, darlin'."

She carefully removed the paper, her face strained with concentration. It became all too apparent in this unguarded moment all of the stress she had been under these last few days. She peeled away the paper, slowly, but deliberately, wanting and not wanting to see what was underneath. Dan hadn't been sure if it was the right thing to do, but he knew what her seeing it would mean, and this had been the worry that plagued him. This secret was not his own, but he hadn't been sure he should be the courier of this one either. But the look on her face as she had it open relaxed all of his tensions. He gazed across at the painting in the frame. A woman riding a horse in the moonlight. "This your work, Sasha?"
She was silent, staring dreamily into it, as if she looked at it hard enough she might be able to fall into it herself. "Yes, Dan. This is mine. It's one of my first works. Where did you get it?"

The tears were streaming down her cheeks, but she didn't look sad. She looked relieved. As if a wave had been looming in the distance, and had just crashed onto the shore. All expectation and worry about the damage the wave could cause was removed. "Where do you think I got it, sugar?" She looked back down at the painting, and from the folds of the paper, she produced a note. He couldn't make out what it said, but it was signed, "All my love, Brandon".

Those startling amethyst eyes peeked back up at him and seemed to ask a question, and even though he wasn't exactly sure what it was, he knew she needed the answer to be 'yes'. He just nodded his head, and said, "Chickadee, there are worse things to be addicted to."

"Oh, Jesus. Jesus, Dan! I've gotta call Justin. I'm sorry, Dan, but I am going to need to go. I promise I will explain it all soon, but I gotta go right now. I've made a big mistake." She jumped up from her chair, and at the same time was furiously punching the numbers on her phone, as she was walking out, he heard her apologizing and saying she was leaving, it had all happened too fast, it was't right, and some other excuses that concealed the whole truth. He stood up, and made his way to the door slowly, but purposefully. He opened it and called out, "Sasha, where are you going, baby girl?" She turned around and looked at him, as if it was the silliest question in the world.

"To the airport, Uncle Dan! I've gotta get back to Detroit. Immediately. I can't explain it all to you now, but I promise I will. But I gotta go!" Just as she was about to close her car door to speed away, Dan laughed and called out another one of the the secrets he had kept under wraps. "Sugar, if you're on your way to find Brandon, you're going the wrong way. He's back at the hotel. And don't worry about doing any explaining, he did all that already. Though I am surprised you'd think he'd let that painting get farther than a few miles from his possession. In my experience, he doesn't let anything he loves get too far away for too long." She rolled her eyes, and strode toward him. She linked her arm in his, leaning her head on his thick motorcycle bomber coat. When she looked back up, he winked at her.

"Okay, take me to him. How did you know, Uncle Dan? How do you always know what I most need?"
"That's what Uncles are for, pumpkin."

She gazed at him softly for a minute, and then looked at him full force with her brilliant purple gaze, her hair lit up like a bonfire by the sun, she looked more like a Celtic warrior queen than his little girl.

"Dan, I'm glad I never knew my father." She definitely had his attention. It was almost like she had divined his other secret, and he was left hopeless and exposed, aching to know her next words, and dreading them too.

"Because, I could never have had a father better than you have been." He smiled, and pulling her closer to him for a moment, walked her over to the truck and opened her door. He opened up the back door and tossed the unopened package, the other secret, into the toolbox in the back of his truck.

As he drove back to the hotel to deliver Sasha to the man that loved her, he felt only happiness. Maybe she knew the truth, maybe she didn't. But he had finally found a place that was as comfortable and safe as his own house, and that was sharing this bench seat with his little girl.

"Danke schoen, darling, danke schoen
Thank you for seeing me again
Though we go on our separate ways
Still the memory stays, for always
My heart says, "Danke schoen"
—Danke Schön, Bert Kaempfert

9 : MUNICH

Reading was probably his greatest pleasure. No matter where they moved, no matter the country or the city, or the friendliness of his new classmates, the books remained the same. The constancy of the friendships he made within the pages, endured.

Whenever he read stories about children being moved from place to place, the books always had the same message. The children wanted a place to settle, they didn't want to be moved around anymore. They would beg and plead with their parents to remain in one spot. Julian couldn't relate with that, he didn't understand what the big deal was. His parents were always moving, and although having to constantly start over in a new place had its challenges, he couldn't imagine any other life. The settled life that the characters in his books yearned for, seemed...boring.

Although he wasn't an overly philosophical child, he had learned something about permanence in his 12 years. He learned that it didn't exist. What he understood was that when you tried to nail something down, it just withered anyway. He didn't even realize he knew this, but the lesson became part of him. So many faces, so many friends, they served a purpose in his life, and he in theirs, and when their time together was over...that was it. He had a vague notion of grandparents and aunts and uncles as being persons connected to him somehow more tightly than friends, but he had only seen any of these people a handful of times. His life then mostly consisted of his mother, his father, his cat Sampson, and boxes and boxes of books.

He had an e-reader for travel, but he agreed with his mother. She had said there was something so much more powerful about reading a book made from paper pages. It wasn't the smell either, even though that's what everyone else said. No, for him and his mother it was something about dog-eared pages, and coming across a smudge from a buttery fingertip, or maybe a bit of jam or dirt that he knew he had put there on his first reading. Or perhaps an underlined word that his mother had marked in the book. It made the pages feel alive. It proved that they had made the journey with him from all of his far off places, like his own heartbeat or a preserved sigh.

His father was an engineer. He worked for an international oil company and had taken an expatriate position. Julian had spent several years thinking that as an engineer, his father worked on cars or drove a train, which had caused his father to laugh rather hard at him for a while, leaving Julian bewildered until an explanation was forthcoming. His mother taught English at international schools. Beyond that, he didn't know anything else about his parent's careers, except that they requested to travel a lot. They didn't ask him how he felt about it, and he never considered that he should feel any certain way.

He was sitting in the railway car on the way to Munich, their new home, re-reading "The Hobbit". He liked to read it when he was in transit. "The Hobbit" or "The Loon Feather" for travel, and "David Copperfield" when he was sad. Like a visit with a friend, he would sit down with Bilbo or Davy and commune with them, hearing their familiar voices on the pages and feel instantly warm all over. He would be transported much farther than any train or plane could take him, which he liked. He liked the idea of going as far away as possible, of escaping into a book and then having to find his way out again.

His guidebooks had said that Munich was clean. It appeared organized, and the descriptions of the city had reminded him of Rotterdam, which they had lived in two years ago. There were few places they had lived that he hadn't cared for, and surprisingly, most of them were in the United States. Everything seemed too new there. He couldn't make sense of the fact that both of his parents had lived there, in the same city, up until they got married. His parents were filled with too much life to be contained in one city. Isn't that always what children felt about their parents, though? Isn't it impossible to ever picture your parents at your own age, trying to make sense of the world? To a child, one's parents were born as they are now, and fitting the two images together results in a blurred negative.

This trip was different though. Julian didn't know it yet, but this was where he would meet Evie. And when they met, everything would change.

For now though, pulling up to the no-nonsense, tall, brick-brown house, Julian felt the same he had felt dozens of times upon entering a new life. He was a feather blown into the wind, never wondering where it is going, or where it may land, but floating along wherever the breeze may take him, enjoying the ride. His parents always seemed extremely thrilled when they were moved somewhere new, and sometimes he felt as though he were the adult and they the children. He loved his parents dreadfully, even if he sometimes wished they were more like the parents of his classmates. Between the two of them, he was fairly confident that his parents knew everything worth knowing about the world. His father could make, draw, create, compose and breathed in numbers, art, and music. His mother was a song of languages, histories and stories.

But, they were not like other parents. He had asked them why they were not, only once, and their reaction had been one of complete and utter bewilderment. It seemed that they really hadn't wanted children, but when it was obvious that they were going to get one, that they resolved to treat him as an equal human being. "Are you a doll, Julian? Are you a little human puppet that we should coddle and dress and coo at? Would you like us to do that, Julian? Your father finds adults that treat children that way appalling. As soon as you were born we could see you were a boy of uncommon good sense, cleverness and sound judgement. We contented ourselves to treat you as someone deserving of love, respect, hugs and good conversation. That is what we have endeavored to do." His mother was brash and outspoken, but he loved her, and he couldn't disagree with the sense of what she said. They didn't own him, and he didn't want them to, but they could all love and care for each other, tied together by companionship and respect. Which may be strange to other families, but, his family was peculiar anyway.

He knew all this to be true, but he still sometimes wished his mother would scold him or his father would yell. If only for the experience. But instead, they all read and they all talked and they all shared their wonderings and ideas. Which would lead Julian to reading more and more, and it scarcely mattered where they were living, as long as there was a wonderful library nearby.

He lugged his suitcases and bags up the stoop of the townhouse, and pushed on the heavy wooden door. His mother was already inside, and his father was making numerous trips back to the taxi. The bulk of their things wouldn't arrive for a few days, so they could all make believe they were on holiday and live out of their suitcases until it arrived. Already though, looking at the exposed brick walls and the scuffed and scratched wooden floor, Julian's mind was racing. He was wondering, which his father said was one of his chief talents. "No one thinks half as deep as you do, Jules, and when it comes to imagination you've got them all beat". He was wondering how many other 12 year old boys had lived here, and what they had been like. He wondered if anyone had ever died in the house and if their ghost still lingered. He wondered if anyone had ever been truly sad here, or if a pretty girl had ever slept in his bedroom. He wondered what type of families had lived in their house and what food they had eaten for dinner on Sundays. He imagined another little boy, his own age, standing in the exact same spot he was in, and he wondered if that boy had ever thought another boy would stand in this spot.

His parents always knew when he was off in his own mind. His eyes would stare ahead, unseeing, and sort of mist over. His mother said that his grey eyes would turn dark, whirlpool blue, and that if you looked closely, you could see the swirl of his thoughts spinning inside of them. Julian didn't know if it was true, but sometimes he wondered what that would look like.

As the days went on, he only found more to wonder about. The kids at his international school were the same as usual. Some of them were interesting, some were not. Many were overwhelmingly common and stupid, whereas others were insipid and didn't seem to have a thought besides the ones occupying their minds at that precise moment. Still others were vaguely intelligent, well spoken and kind. He did not seek any of them out, he did not need to. Julian knew that eventually they would find him, and they would either like him or not, despite his trying or lack of trying, and then he would most probably be gone not too long after. It didn't make him sad, it just made him tired.

But one day, a few weeks in, riding his bike the short distance to the school, he drove past a little blonde girl that he knew he had seen in classes. Her movements seemed to be equal parts dance, float, and walk. She was clutching some books to her chest, and when he passed by and looked at her, she winked. There was nothing remarkable about her. She looked like a hundred other little girls his age. The curling blonde hair, the baby-fat angel face with pink lips and long lashes. But it wasn't her appearance that caught his eye, it was the books. She was holding them the way he held his own. As if she were holding a friend's hand or protecting a newborn kitten. Gently, yet with courage. He felt, in that wink, in that moment, a kindred spirit.

He couldn't help being more aware of her as the days went on. He observed her habits, searching for a reason to stop noticing her. Something that would label her ordinary again, so that he could fold back into his books and his interests. But the more he saw, the more intrigued he became. Her name was Evie, and she sat alone at lunch as he did. She sat away from the class in a desk in the corner. She didn't talk to anyone, never raised her hand, and seemed to be always reading under the desk, or at anytime she had a free moment. He was spellbound.

At home, his parents had been settling into their new jobs, taking him to see the glockenspiel, and the museums. They had gone to Ammersee and taken a tour of the lake in a boat surrounded on all sides by the majesty of German countryside. They had driven all through the small Bavarian villages, which seemed like places from the settings of all of his fairytales. Each small town appearing more idyllic than the one before.

Julian wasn't sure when exactly they had started their companionship. He didn't remember saying hello, or introducing himself. It seemed to him that one day he sat by her at lunch and that was all it needed. As soon as it began it was an easy, comfortable bond. He wasn't in love with her, he knew that for sure; he had only been in love once, and quite recently. His poor heart was still bruised with the rejection. She had been his Italian tutor, and when he had gotten the courage to propose, she had told him that as charming as his offer was, they were both far too young to be married.

She had kissed him on the cheek, and his heart had bled all through the rest of their lessons together.

No, it wasn't love. It was something rarer. Not unlike the feeling of laying on the grass in the summer. Your own heart is pressed up to the heartbeat of the earth, there is a natural connection there. A connection so deep that to be any closer you would have to be swallowed up by it. That's how it felt with Evie. He really didn't have any words to define it, except to say that they seemed to need each other. To belong in companionship. And for the first time, he didn't make it something to sit and wonder about. He just accepted it. Her voice was the sweet sound of a hesitant piano player's fingers on the keys. Clear, but soft. An old song playing on a record through the too-thin walls of the flat upstairs. You had to really focus on the words to hear them.

Evie would light up like a flame when Julian brought her books to read, greeting each one like it was person she had longed to meet her whole life. Julian liked that about her, because he felt the same way about the books she brought him. She brought him fantastic books of enchantment, and potions, and flying carpets and lands that never were. He brought her histories, and novels, and books about how things worked and why they were made. They would piece all of the genres together sitting back to back, looking over each other's shoulders at the books they were both reading, and discussing how they pictured it all.

She hadn't lived in Munich all her life, but she couldn't remember where she'd lived before very well. Her father had been stationed here in the military, and because she had family in Germany, her parents were more than glad to remain. Evie said she'd been here as long as she could remember, "and sometimes even before that", she'd add, smiling.
"What's it like? Staying in just one place?"
"But, I don't. I travel just as much as you do."
"Huh? You just said..."

They were walking into Marienplatz, Evie linked her arm through Julian's and looked at him with an impish grin that lit up her angel face. "Did you know that it is a beast that wakes up the dancers in the glockenspiel every day at 11?"

He turned to shove her off for teasing him as the clock began to strike, and a movement caught his eye. His face turned upwards and he saw it. A great, hairy beast was tapping each of the figures to begin their dance. His clumsy claws tapped at them nervously as he anxiously looked down at the crowd of people below him. The dancers all transformed from life size figurines into real people, their dress a glittering, vibrant mass of movement and color. "How...?"
"The people below can't see him because they aren't looking for him, just like you weren't until a moment ago. And they can't see the dancers because all they expect to see is clockwork. And so they do". She spoke as if it was all so perfectly logical that there could be no contradicting it. Her grin had turned into a full smile. "Catch me!"

Julian ran after her as she fled the Marienplatz and onto Tal. She turned her head and called out to him in that soft snowflake voice, "I hope you can swim!" and within a matter of moments, Julian no longer heard the dull thud of his shoes on the grey Munich street, but instead his legs kicked out behind him and his arms paddled out front as the city filled with water, deeper and deeper, the water climbed over the windows, over the roofs. Sampson floated by in his cat bed, still softly dozing, and all at once the world was blue. Julian's eyes widened in amazement and he treaded water, turning in a circle and looking about him. He was reminded of a time in Mexico when he had gone deep sea fishing with his father, and realizing that they were so far from land that he couldn't even see a single grain of sand on the horizon. He filled with that same excitement and dread now, but didn't have time to worry, as Evie appeared in a small sailboat and pulled him on deck. He was dry in a moment, as if he had never been in the water at all.

"How? Did you? But...how?!" Julian stammered out. Evie just smiled. "I don't need trains or planes or ships to travel." She said. Her eyes were laughing, but not at him.

"Is Munich... magic?" He asked, feeling silly but marveling all the same.

"No, but my imagination *is*." She answered in perfect earnestness. They were staring deeply into each other's eyes, and he felt that he had always known her, and that her secrets were not secrets at all to him. But instead, forgotten truths. The finding of an old letter you had written as a child to discover you were much wiser than you were now. He looked down, expecting to see the boards of the boat underneath him, but instead seeing the familiar grey of the streets, and his ears filled with the rough German syllables of the locals. He looked about him as the Schäfflertanz, the cooper's dance, was just ending on the great clock. Had they been standing in this spot for the full twelve minutes of the show? Or had they been riding the waves on a sailboat from a dream that happened, but also couldn't have? Julian didn't know, and Julian didn't wonder. But somehow he knew that for all of the countries he had seen and the cities he had lived in, that he hadn't really been anywhere. He had just scratched the surface of the real adventures of his life.

Thus began their journeys. Munich came alive when he was with Evie. She would take his hand and they were paddling a skiff through a sticky sweet river of honey, or teaching Sampson to speak German with the other cats. Birds flew down from the sky and carried them for a view of the city before dropping them off at the doors of the school. Apples grew out of buildings and trees produced pancakes. After a time he would take her hand and they would be trekking through the sands of Egypt and gazing at the pyramids. They walked through the halls of the Louvre in which hung all of the paintings Julian liked best, even the ones that he knew were at the National Gallery or the Met. They would walk down a street in which every flat, house, or bungalow he had ever lived in was lined up in a row. He would take her into each one and show her around. Soon he could change Munich at will, sometimes when out shopping with his mother, or when he was bored in class. But, it was always better to slip into that secret Munich when they were together, as if it came more vibrantly to life when they both were there.

He never saw her talk to anyone else, and had felt very strange when her family had come for dinner at his house and she hadn't said a word. Instead she had just squeezed his hand under the table, and gave him that same wink that she had given him the day he had first noticed her. But, he was happy. And for a while he forgot to long for new places. He forgot to wonder about where they would go next. He didn't even have to wonder how many boys his age had lived in their house or if a beautiful girl had lived in his room. He saw them all now as he came home from school, and blushed when he woke up and saw the girl sleeping in the twin bed by the window. He didn't have to wonder, because he saw. He had borrowed Evie's eyes, and through them the world was a very different place.

But, inevitably, it came time for them to move on. He didn't fight his parents or throw a fit, deep down he didn't really want to settle. It was not in his nature just as much as it wasn't in theirs. His heart hurt though, at the thought of leaving Evie, and she'd come to his house the night before he was to leave to say goodbye. They sat in the living room and stared straight upward. A passerby might have thought it strange to see two children staring at the ceiling, but no one passed. They weren't staring at the ceiling though, but at the stars. And not from Munich, but sitting on top of the Empire State Building. They promised to write to each other, but Julian knew it would probably not last long. They'd send a few letters and then they'd grow bored of it. Staying in touch wasn't important, the time they had together here had been. It had changed him, opening his eyes to the infinite, and his own smallness in the world.

On the plane the next morning, Julian felt his mother's gaze on him over his book. He put it down on his lap for a moment, and she laid down hers as well. His father was snoring softly in the next seat, despite numerous protestations that he was "Wide awake, couldn't sleep a wink".

"Ahh, David Copperfield. Someone is feeling a little down, eh?"

"I guess."

His mother offered him a weak smile, and sighed before she spoke. "I wanted to tell you, Jules, I know Evie was special to you, and we thought it was very kind of you to be her friend."

Julian gave his mother a bemused look. "Uh, it was no problem. She was easy to talk to. Ya know? I felt like she understood me."

Now it was his mother's turn to look confused. "Is that a joke, Julian?"

Julian's eyes narrowed and he tilted his head. "What are you talking about, Mom?"

Still looking at him strangely, his mother continued, "Julian...we both know that Evie can't talk. She's mute."

"What? What are you saying? That's ridiculous."

His mother seemed a little exasperated as she continued, "Julian, honey, her mother told us all about it the night her family came to dinner." She paused, waiting for Julian to speak, and when he didn't she went on, "She doesn't talk at school, she doesn't have friends, the teacher never calls on her for answers. She doesn't talk. Period. Now, I know that you're a sweet guy and that you have a big imagination, but I think you can admit that you noticed she's a little quiet." His mother was giving him a cocked eyebrow and eyeing him sidelong.

Julian stared ahead, horrified. For it had suddenly dawned on him that although he could hear her clear, musical voice in his mind perfectly, he couldn't remember ever seeing her mouth move. Or ever hearing her laugh. Only that same smile. "But..."

His mother had settled back into her book, but dropping it a few inches she added, "I figured you were just reading her like you do your books." The thought hung in the air.

"Sometimes the words you hear in the voice of your mind matter more anyway. Don't you think?" And before he could respond the book was back up in front of her face, and he knew the conversation was over. He leaned toward the window, and watched the clouds turn into a sea of rolling foam, and for a moment saw Evie waving at him from a sailboat, smiling. He felt the corner of his mouth curve upward, and a single raindrop escaped from the storm of his grey eyes, and he knew that if he could see them, they would be a whirlpool of blue.

"It's an odd thing, but anyone who disappears is said to be seen in San Francisco. It must be a delightful city and possess all the attractions of the next world."
—Oscar Wilde

10 : SAN FRANCISCO

It's hard to walk around with so much hate inside of you all the time. To be filled with hate like a bucket of water, brimming and filled and sloshing around. And it never fully goes away. It just twists and reshapes itself into a different type of hate. The truth was, I had wanted her to die. I guess not die, but I had wished she had never been. I wondered what life would have been like if she hadn't been born, if it was just me.

Even so, I did love Miranda. A piece of me had to, everyone did. How could you not? She was kind, sweet, and radiant. She was helpful and considerate, always putting the happiness of other's before her own. I loved her, but I hated her too. And I hated myself for it.

I really can't think of a time I didn't secretly despise her. Even when we were small and playing with our dolls, and she would let me have the prettiest one, or the newest one, and I would well up with hatred at her thoughtfulness. It wasn't that our parents didn't like me, it was just...they loved Miranda more. And I resented that too, because I understood why. She was filled with love, and I was filled with hate.

For a long time I felt like it was a fate that was affixed to me, like my eye color or a birthmark. She was the favorite, I was the black sheep. She was meant to do, and achieve, and charm everyone she met, and I was meant for smaller, meaner things. That the die had been cast long ago, and I had somehow lost the game without ever knowing I was playing.

Of course, everything changed when she committed suicide. It was the first frozen raindrop of the storm of secrets that followed; she had been pregnant, her boyfriend didn't know, she had lost the baby, he had rejected her not knowing about the baby, and then she destroyed herself. When I write it like that, it doesn't seem to hold the same power, does it? Yet, this is the chain of circumstances that led to my sister putting our father's 9mm to her head, and pulling the trigger. Unbelievable that, *Miranda the sweet, Miranda the good,* was ever that unhappy. That hopeless. But she was. I am unable to even imagine the depth of feeling that would lead to a decision like that. Which is why that the day that she killed herself, was the day I stopped hating her. It was the day I started loathing myself.

Hate begets hate, and so I have lived now in a dark world of festering anger. At myself, at my parents and at Miranda.

Last summer my parents were in a serious car accident, which thankfully, left them unhurt. It did serve as a wake-up call, however, a brush with mortality for Mom and Dad. Mom started calling more, and bugging me about seeing her, and visiting, and perhaps having a mother-daughter trip. I had resisted going for a long time. I had put it out of my mind and ignored my mother's pleas. But, I had come home and found my bag already packed. My boss had stopped in my office and offered me the week off. A friend said they had heard I might be leaving and offered to watch my cat. As if someone was behind the scenes pulling the strings. As if it had all been planned. All I could think was that a guardian angel or a ghost had set it all up, and I had no excuses not to go this time. And so, this is why I find myself pretending to sleep in my own queen size bed across from my mother at the Omni Hotel in San Francisco.

Pretending to sleep. Yes. I hoped you would catch that. My mother and I met here at the hotel on Monday afternoon, as we had flown in from different cities. I hadn't been too excited to meet at all, as I prefer to be alone with my anger and my career, and to stay away from past memories as much as possible; but something in her voice this time told me I had to come. But I can't shake the feeling that the same force that sent me on this trip, has also somehow traveled with me and met up with us here. And if it wasn't ridiculously crazy, I'd say it was Miranda.

That's insane isn't it? But I could have sworn I felt her hand in mine when Mom and I were looking for a coffee shop, I heard her laugh when we were grabbing a glass of wine before dinner. I felt her...hovering between us. I could almost see her smile. And as much as I hate to admit it... I liked it. It was the first time I'd been happy in years. Crazy? Yes. It's like the anger was being lifted off of me like a heavy cloak, as if I had no idea how much lighter I could be, as if I was floating away in happiness with it. We hadn't discussed it, but Mom seemed different too. Less... dejected, less melancholy, why, her face lit up almost like it used to for Miranda. And when she smiled, I felt the press of Miranda's hand in mine, a squeeze of love that caused a surge of forgiveness...for myself? For Miranda? I had felt the phantom of her sorrow haunting me all of these years, but what if it was my own mourning that haunted me? And that this specter of love is her *real* ghost?

I opened my eyes and sat up, unable to feign sleep any longer and when I looked over, I saw my mother, softly crying in her own bed. For some reason, the right thing was to get up and climb in next to her, like I had wanted to after Miranda died. Like I had wanted to a hundred times and never had the courage, because I thought she didn't want me. But she did now. She grasped my hand, and words flowed from her, swirling and rolling like the tide. It was words that I had longed to hear, and words I never thought I would, words about her sadness, words about her own anger. To hear that she had been angry too! She had been angry at Miranda, and at herself. She had felt alone and cut off, as I too, had felt. And then, the words stopped. She looked at me as if seeing me for the first time.

"Cassandra, would you like to grab some lunch? I've just realized I'm famished". When I agreed and began to stand up, I felt arms that I hadn't even known were there un-clasp from around me, arms that were familiar to me. Arms that could only have been Miranda's. The ghostly feeling was gone the moment I felt it, though, and we busied ourselves getting dressed. It was late afternoon, but we had been having a long lie-in after lunch. We decided that all we wanted was some fresh sourdough, straight from an oven somewhere, and perhaps a strong cup of coffee, and so to the Ferry Building we headed on foot.

My mother is a prodigious walker. She was known throughout the neighborhood for her pace and her resolution when taking a constitutional. All our lives, Miranda had been the only one who could keep up with her, and I had always lagged behind. But today, either she had slowed down, or someone had quickened my feet, but we were perfectly in-step.

In Grand Rapids, where I live, the city moves faster. The people seem busier. I'm so occupied at the law office that I have no time to look at the buildings, to meet new people, to enjoy a stroll anywhere... and my life is fueled by regret and caffeine. How long had I been this way? I don't know. I felt that I was a finished copy, and that I was preset to be unhappy, so I always had been. But strolling along next to mom, I saw the years on her face. Here was a woman who had raised two daughters, one who was as sweet as sunshine, and the other as unknown as the night, and filled with as many terrors. She had been the one who had walked in on Miranda that last day, and she was the one who would carry that image around with her forever. Her perfect wish of a girl was dead, and all that was left was me. I started to slow my feet, but I felt a reassuring arm link through mine that kept me moving forward. The whole trip had gone strange. What was this? Ghostly phantasms? Dead sisters come back to life, as kind dead as they had been alive? I sighed and walked on.

We reached The Mill on foot and wandered in to find some fresh bread, grab some coffee, and found a bench that looked out onto the street and streetcars, old and new. We tore off chunks of the still-warm loaf, and gazed down the dollhouse San Francisco streets that reminded me of a favorite 90's sitcom. We sat there companionably for a while, discussing the city and our impressions of our spooky night tour of Alcatraz, and the scallops we had gorged on at dinner the night before. We talked about watching the sunset over the Golden Gate, and the way the sun seemed brighter here as it glanced off the friendly water. I was struck by the ease of the conversation. Why had I avoided my parents so completely? Why had I thought they didn't like me? Why did I believe that I hated them?

I began to cry. Softly at first, but then a torrent. I felt my mother's hand creep around my clenched right fist, and I felt someone smoothing my hair. And I knew. She was there, or her love was, and it had been there all the time. All the years I had spent hating her, hating myself, hating my parents... they didn't matter. Because she had forgiven me before I ever needed to be. It was a strange revelation, in fact, this whole trip had been like a ghostly dream. The unexpected phone call from Mom, the immediate remembrances of Miranda... I felt for a moment like it had all been predestined, as if all of the events of my life had been leading up to this moment of revelation and absolution. Just as I was going to express this to my mother, she turned and said, "Let's jump on the next bus and head for Crissy Field, I'd like to watch that sunset."

A half hour later we found ourselves standing, staring out into the bay, the enormous gleaming bridge jutting out of the water, confidently. The sky was cotton candy and lilacs, and every wave in the water seemed to carry the bitterness and spite away from deep within me. I breathed easier, and a closeness to my mother crept over me that I had never felt. An opening of spirit, or perhaps the first time I had allowed myself to be vulnerable. Miranda's ghostly presence was still discernible, but it was warmth and succor instead of vaguely vexing. It gave me courage.

"Mom, about that day..."
"What day, Cassie?"

"The day...the day that you found her body. The day she killed herself. I've always wanted to ask you about it...but, it's okay if you can't talk about it. I understand."

She slowly turned away from the flamingo-pink reflection of the last rays of the sun on the water, and looked at me. I kept my eyes toward the bridge, not trusting myself to look back at her. Loath to ruin this new found amity between us.

"It doesn't bother me, sweetheart. The scene has haunted me for so many years, that it has fairly lost its power. I'm afraid there isn't much to say, though." She paused here for a moment and breathed out heavily before continuing on.
"There was blood. A lot of it. I never knew there was so much in a person. I could barely reconcile what I was seeing, Cass. But at the same time, I had always known. Your Dad and I always knew that Miranda was...fragile. She was glass to your iron. We always feared she would break...such a gentle, delicate girl."

I wasn't sure how to react. I had always taken her kindness as a form of strength...but my parents had seen her differently. She had said that I was 'iron' as if it was a compliment. I'm not sure why, but I brightened to hear it.

"Our little Irish twins. 11 months apart! You know, we always thought you would be inseparable, but we were glad you weren't. Right from the beginning, you were so...independent. She was always hugging, always smiling, always helping. Not you. No, you were always stronger. Self-reliant. Steely. Resolute. We were so proud of you both, but there was always a whisper of worry for Miranda. We were never nervous about you. We knew you'd take care of yourself, and you have...look at you, Cass! Successful, settled, well-traveled. I just wish I had seen more of you. We both do. But, after Miranda...well, we just let things run their course."

She paused, and I felt hot prickles of shame on my face. Proud! They were proud? They had left me alone because they trusted me more? They had found fault with Miranda? I was dumbfounded. My whole life, all that I had believed to be true was being shaken from its very foundations. I had never imagined that my parents, that anyone, had ever seen Miranda as somehow...*less* than me. But, even amongst these discoveries, I knew I still had a few questions. The questions that had tormented me for the past seven years. One question that had just about burned me up in the flames of self-doubt, and self-hate.

"Mom, that day. When you walked in and found her..."
"Yes...?"

"Did you...Did you ever wish it was me instead?"

The words were out. They were out of my mouth, they had escaped. I felt in that moment that I had ruined it. That she would have no choice but to say yes. To admit that she would rather have lost me than her darling girl.

"Oh, Cassie. Honey, No. I wish it was *me*."

Without thought or hesitation I brought my eyes to hers, and in them saw an eternity of longing. Of love. Of regret. But not regret that I had lived, regret that she had outlived her daughter. Regret that it was not me and Miranda on this trip together, trading remembrances of *her*. I felt the ghostly brush of feathery lips on my cheek. Warm and cold at the same time. It was the last time I would ever feel my sister, though I have come to think about her often since, and about what it had meant to have a sister that I never understood until it was too late.

As we watched the golden coil sink from sight, and the water become wild and cerulean, I asked her my final question. Did she think it had all been predestined? Was Miranda meant to die? Was that why she was born so loving? Were we meant to be here like this, missing her? My mother kissed me on the forehead, and I knew it was something I would have to answer myself.

The next day, we left San Francisco, moving in different directions at the airport. There was a warmth between us that hadn't been there before, a closeness that had fought its way to the surface and settled in. We parted fondly, and as I sat down to wait for my flight, I felt the urge to call her already, somehow immediately missing my mother. The sky was cloaked in a smoky fog, and it was strange to think that the haze outside was more tangible than my sister, lying in her grave, yet surrounding us.

Everyone says things happen for a reason, but I am now of the belief that nothing does. My sister did not kill herself as part of a great plan, and I have not held onto hate all of this time because it was preordained. All is coincidence and chance. The sheer infinite number of catastrophes and triumphs that could befall us at any one moment, and how in our mean, small, scared, human life we either shrink or rise to those circumstances... this makes a life. It is not an orchestrated play, but a dazzling, spinning chaos of love and hate and all things in between.

I believe we are our own. To rise, to fall, to blunder or create victory. And all of the obstacles or opportunities that fall onto our path are ours alone. To meet with defeat or ultimate triumph is but mere chance; but no matter what one must face on their path, the manner in which you embrace this marvelous, terrible life creates or destroys real happiness.

Live. Breathe. Rejoice. Travel. That is enough.

AFTERWORD

What is said about books is that we read to know that we are not alone. And so, what began as a book about beautiful, exciting places, turned quickly into a character study, a glimpse into the lives of other people. The momentous events in their lives that may mean nothing to an observer, but can be crushing or life-altering for those experiencing it. It is, after all, the people that make a place, and not the other way around. An abandoned house or castle may be fascinating to walk around in, but not because of the place itself, but because of our imaginings of the lives of those that lived there.

The human existence is an experience and expression of humanity, and I find that the more that I travel, the more I am faced with the fact that we are all basically striving towards the same things. That our worries are universal. Contentment and dissatisfaction are bedfellows every place on Earth. A heartbreak in Miami hurts just as bad as one in Stuttgart. People shut themselves off from the world just as much in Amsterdam as in Belize. People the world over find themselves middle-aged and living a life that is not their own, in a loveless marriage with children they don't know. These are not all life and death issues, but they are *our* issues. They are the fears and triumphs of the planet. They may not kill us, but they *can* be numbered in the reasons to continue to live.

So, it is with those thoughts in mind that I wrote this book. It is all real. The characters are not and the stories are not, but all of the stories are my stories, or the stories of those I have met on my travels. They are my friend's stories, or my family's. I have twisted and turned each side of human joy and disappointment, and hope that I offered readers a glimpse into a life that is not their own, but could be. Into the life of someone you know now, or may have yet to meet. On a train, in a bar, or dancing in the piazza on the Amalfi Coast. A reminder that we are separated by oceans and countries, streets and languages...but we are all struggling and celebrating the same.

Bon voyage.

ABOUT THE AUTHOR

Alexandria Nolan is the author of
"Paradise of Exiles" a travel memoir, and
"Shears of Fate" a historical fiction novel. She
maintains a lifestyle blog,
Greetings from Nolandia, and is a frequent
contributor to various online and print
publications.

She resides in Houston, Texas with her husband,
Terrence, and a menagerie of spoiled pets.

www.greetingsfromnolandia.com

www.ingramcontent.com/pod-product-compliance
Lightning Source LLC
Chambersburg PA
CBHW021046130626
46552CB00005B/2040